GW00579432

DARK MIRRORS

DARK MIRRORS

A NOVEL OF PROVENCE

GUSTAF SOBIN

BLOOMSBURY

First published 1992
Copyright © 1992 by Gustaf Sobin
The moral right of the author has been asserted
Bloomsbury Publishing Ltd, 2 Soho Square, London W1V 5DE

A CIP catalogue record for this title is available
from the British Library

ISBN 0 7475 1168 3

10 9 8 7 6 5 4 3 2 1

Typeset by Hewer Text Composition Services, Edinburgh
Printed and bound in Great Britain by
Mackays of Chatham PLC, Chatham, Kent

For my brother, *Harris*, with love and lasting gratitude

1

On the last night of his life, Guy Fallows dreamt of pigeons. The pigeons, huddled in the lee of the ridge-tiles of a tall, stucco farmhouse, sheltered themselves – as well as they could – against a high, luminous, unabating mistral, overhead. One occasionally would flutter down into the dust-blown farmyard below. There, it would sprinkle itself in whatever water it found in any of the stout little basins, scattered about. The basins – troughs, really – gouged out of field-stone, reminded Guy Fallows, even in his dream, of so many grey, lopsided pumpkins. He looked on, fascinated. He felt as if he were attending a private show, an exclusive viewing of some minor, agrarian activity that could – at any instant – turn into something deeply significant. Yes, he thought, at any given instant, this flickering dream scenery could, without notice, take on a depth – an unsuspected meaning – entirely its own.

Now as he peered, a privileged spectator into that very dream, the same pigeon – shivering, bright white – rose up and regained its perch overhead amongst the speckled, red roof-tiles. There, it shook from its feathers the last, scavenged drops of trough water. The drops, spinning in perfect half-wheels off the pigeon's body, caught – incendiary – in the late afternoon light. For only the briefest instant, they seemed to freeze – in mid-air – like

1

so many thin, vermilion needles. Then, just as quickly, vanished – as if evaporated – into the gathering dusk.

'Guido,' Guy Fallows whispered, called out from the depth of his dream.

'Guido, Guido,' he murmured, addressing no one really but the husked syllables of a name, hoping perhaps to call at least the name's attention – the empty vocable's – to the pigeons, perched on the roof.

There, facing northwards, with their white feathers ruffled, they shifted, one against the other, tense from what the wind, in Provence, instils in each living creature. While one preened, another would tug, shove, squabble for place. Then, frenetic, as if directed by some common but thoroughly covert signal, they'd all, simultaneously, take flight. They'd rise, and – blown southward – scatter like seed. Like shrapnel. Gathering altitude as they did, they'd then regroup into a single cloud, obeying – it would seem – a single, imperceptible volition. Fallows, looking on or rather *in* upon this improvised spectacle, this endless filmstrip of flight and displacement, followed the birds as if they themselves might serve – like stars, or tea-leaves, or yarrow stalks – to indicate fortune. Might, if read properly, give Guy Fallows a sign, a tiny, overlooked, even arcane indication – on that last night of his life – of some yet unsuspected reprieve.

Now, blown over a thicket of dwarf oak and aleppo, the pigeons vanished into one of those wastelands called, in that region, a *garrigue*. Fallows – suddenly – felt at a loss. The very agents that had animated his dream had just as if volatilized. Like so many ephemeral spirits, they'd vanished. (Hadn't they, in reality, disappeared altogether, Fallows might have pondered. Within the Provençal landscape, weren't pigeons now nearly extinct? Hadn't they become, along with so much else, as if vestigial? Relics of a lost economy, a dilapidated order? Guy Fallows himself

2

might well have remembered how ten, twelve years earlier, every farmhouse, every *mas*, had its dovecote. And, from whichever direction one approached that *mas*, one would be greeted by those white, fluttering bouquets. By the muffled thunder of all that wingbeat. He'd always been amazed, in fact, how so much brightness could rise, buoyant, over those low, sombre farmhouses where, even at noon, the shutters would be fastened shut, and wine, darker than the vaulted cellars in which it was kept, would be drawn off in a trickle that more resembled some narrow, uncut length of black string, or thread.)

Once again, they'd returned. Wings tucked forward, tail feathers fanned, the pigeons entered, in Guy Fallows's dream, an orchard of flowering cherries. The trees, suddenly, glowed even brighter. It's spring, Guy Fallows whispered, astonished. Thank heavens, it's still only spring, he added, as – white on white – the pigeons (like so many game birds in some medieval fresco, illustrating abundance) glided beneath the orchard's low, overhanging branches. The branches – in the heavy wind – bobbed and heaved. On them, the blossoms, like so many white coral bracelets, shivered with each successive gust.

'Guido,' Guy whispered. 'Look, look, it's still spring,' he silently exuded. 'Still only spring.'

Each time Guy evoked Guido's name, the pigeons – the dream pigeons, that is – flew, it seemed, even faster. It was as if their metabolism itself had been charged by the simple enunciation of those two syllables. As if, instantaneously, the mere mention of Guido's name had pumped life, and massively, into their very system.

Climbing now, they flew – an octave unto themselves – against the violet-grey ridge-line of the Luberon. Here and there, a stone village, like a lost chord, lay perched upon its rock outcropping. Or occasionally the gaping wound of a lime quarry – like a white fracture – would show itself against the deep and sombre folds of the long mountain. Guy Fallows realized that he was being treated, in his dream, to a sweeping panorama of that part of Provence he'd lived in now for over twenty years. That, on the last night of his life, the pigeons were guiding him across the landscape of his very own memory.

Now, banking in a slow half-circle, they came to settle – one by one – in a young wheatfield, just before him. The wind marbled the surface of the wheat silver, brushing it smooth in so many long, dissolving swaths. There, the pigeons strutted and pecked, strutted and pecked, their ruffled heads just visible over the top of the seething grain.

'Spring,' Guy Fallows continued to whisper, utterly amazed. 'Time, there's still time, Guido,' he went on, marvelling at his own good fortune. Exulting, from the depth of his dream, how he'd managed, at least, to postpone the irreparable.

'Yes, still only spring.' And, just as he said this, the flock, startled no doubt by a sudden gust of wind, took flight once again. They arose as one, then – dragged by the mistral downwind – flew in a tattered formation southward. Guy Fallows followed them in his dream as far as Lacoste (*his* village, he liked to call it) and to the terraces, just below, where beehives glinted – in the late afternoon sunlight – a flat, acid white. There, just then, the pigeons began to circle.

'Guido, Guido,' he whispered, trying to call his attention, perhaps, to some detail in the landscape: to the beehives, perhaps, or the castle of Lacoste – de Sade's – standing as it does like a gigantic, cracked molar on its hillside. 'Guido,' he called out, addressing no one, in fact, he'd ever known. No one, materially, he could have ever encountered. For Guido, Guido Stampelli, had passed away long before Guy Fallows had arrived in those hills. He'd died, in fact, over forty years earlier, leaving neither offspring nor property;

4

leaving nothing, in reality, but the signature of a few, scattered farmhouses that he'd built with his own hands. But stables, tool-sheds, a fountainhead – here and there – and, most of all, a *pigeonnier* he'd reconstructed for Marguerite St Chamas that had so thoroughly captivated Guy Fallows's imagination that he'd made of Guido – of Guido's name, that is – a kind of grace word.

'Look. Look, Guido. They're circling,' he whispered. 'Over there, just there,' he indicated. One might easily imagine that, even from the depth of his dream, Guy's lips must have moved. Must have rounded to the 'G' in 'Guido'. Must have pressed – dental – to the 'd' before entering the long, endlessly open suspiration of the 'o'.

'Just there,' Guy Fallows gestured to his near namesake (to what he might have called, in fact, his 'breath-sake'). 'There, to the left,' he specified, because, at that very moment, he could see that the pigeons were preparing to settle. Were lofting, almost motionlessly now, over that very dovecote Guido had not only reconstructed, but slept in – night after night – both as its architect and day-labourer, wrapped in a horse blanket and lying on whatever straw he'd managed to sweep together in that lower room of two rooms, designed, in reality, as a rabbit hutch and where, perhaps, Guido himself might have whispered to some such 'breath-sake'. Might have directed his anguish, the tiny, breath-bitten increments of his whispers, in the direction – who can say – of some absentee of his own.

Now the pigeons, in mid-air, seemed as if anchored. The oncoming mistral had grown so massive, so unrelenting, that the birds – held as if tethered in wind – had to calculate their landing, now, faultlessly. Once again, moving as one, rising altogether like a white handkerchief pinched, at its very corner, by a pair of invisible fingers, they climbed, and – in the very same gesture – plummeted, relapsed, came to alight, almost daintily, on the speckled red roof-tiles of the dovecote.

Fallows, now, in his dream, saw nothing but white. But their white wings and fanned tail feathers as they entered into the endless, endlessly minor accommodations that pigeons make – one with the next – fluttering and settling, fluttering and settling as they do. White over white, white under and against and between so many flapping remiges of white, they came – in his closely focused dream – to form a wall, a solid rampart of white. Of luminous, white wingbeats.

Then, that very instant, the white as if roared. And Fallows, in response, rolled over in his sleep on to the far side of an empty bed. The very same wind that had blown all night through his dream – keeping the pigeons aloft and marbling the green wheat silver – blew now, and forcibly, through that transparent wall that separates sleep from wakefulness. Gradually, Fallows stirred. Lying there, eyes still closed, he listened to the shutters in his empty bedroom rattle on their loose hooks. He began to distinguish, bit by bit, the sound the grape leaves made, brushing against the outside wall, from that of the flanking cypresses. For the leaves whispered, even hissed, whereas the cypresses rasped. He listened, astonished that the same wind that had literally transpierced his dream, shredding its way through that white rampart, was blowing, now, with perfect consistency, in the first dark light of dawn, just outside.

Guy Fallows, fully conscious, awoke now to that very day he'd spent so much of his adult life dreading. Certainly, as an artist, he'd harboured an almost speculative curiosity as to its true nature, but awaking now to that small dawn before him, he closed his eyelids in nearly the very same instant he opened them. He lay there now, and listened to his own breathing. Listened to his every breath. Then, testing that tiny mechanism whereby the eyelids open and close with such ease, such seeming autonomy, he opened them once again, and saw – across the tiled floor – his own body, reflected in the bedroom mirror. Wrapped in so many twisted, white sheets, the body, the bulk of his body, seemed to float – almost buoyant – across the mirror's full, unwavering length.

Guy Fallows, once again, closed his eyes, clamped them shut. And, as he did, he felt his eyelids – this time – bunch into a tight network of nerves. He lay there now in his own dark. He lay there – eyes shut – and didn't dare look.

2

'It's hers,' he said.

'Whose?' Guy Fallows asked, somewhat impatiently. The two of them, several months earlier, had been hiking down a narrow footpath that ran – like a beige ribbon – through black ilex and glistening, knee-high clumps of flowering boxwood. Occasionally, a warbler, startled by their footsteps, would plunge into an even deeper thicket, just ahead. For the most part, though, the *garrigue* about them, as they themselves, remained perfectly – almost oppressively – silent. They seemed, in fact, to be walking in the very draught of that silence as they came now to a low, overhanging ledge, and spotted – just below – the tall farmhouse. It lay, obviously abandoned, in a sprawling, grey and rose coloured mass, overrun with bramble and dappled by the shade of so many broad, five-fingered fig leaves.

'No, maybe it's not hers,' the young man whispered, correcting himself. 'Maybe it's her mother's. Yes, that's it,' he added, 'it's her mother's, I'm fairly certain.'

Ever since he'd first learnt to talk, Andrew had expressed himself with what Guy Fallows qualified, a bit testily, as an 'inveterate vagueness'. He didn't so much define his thoughts as diffuse them. He let each and every phrase bleach, go edgeless, lose all precision whatsoever

8

for the sake of a particular, even a distinctive sort of approximation. For creating, about his least remark, the mildest, most impalpable aura possible.

'Whose? Whose mother?' Guy insisted.

The young man concentrated on the narrow footpath before him. 'Vic told me something about it belonging, once, to *her* mother, or perhaps to her mother's mother, if I'm not mistaken.' Then added, as a final qualifier, 'It's either one or the other, though. Of that, I'm nearly certain.' He kept his eyes fixed on the ground before him.

Within minutes, the two of them had reached the outlying walls of the large farmhouse. Its low, dark, north-facing façade appeared as if masoned in ivy: in those wild veinings that – rampant – not only followed but replaced the mortar, running as they did between the grey, loaf-shaped field-stones themselves. There, exposed to the wind, only a few thin-slitted windows interrupted the wall's otherwise blind surface. Squat and somewhat cambered, the wall itself – as if wired in ivy – seemed twice rooted to the ground it stood on.

The other side was something else. Guy Fallows and his son came about now, and entered – through a basket-handle archway – its enclosed courtyard. Over them stood the tall, south-facing façade with its double tier of vaulted windows. Each of the windows lay flanked by an equally tall, exhausted pair of teal-blue shutters. All of it – windows, shutters, and the high, rose stucco frontage – stood as if facing (like some kind of discarded stage décor) the memory of so many spent, agrarian suns.

Crossing the wide flagstones of what once had been a threshing floor, they entered (Guy through one open door; his son, Andrew, through another) the long-since deserted household. Inside, in the sudden dark, each of them must have felt assailed by the place's utter dereliction.

9

Everything within (designed two, three centuries earlier with such rigorous intent as to its specific function) had fallen into total disuse. Nothing, any longer, served. Only the gutted volumes, occasionally, stood witness to the farmhouse's once flourishing economy. Wandering about as they did, they began to read those gutted volumes, those abandoned shells. They began deducing, or simply guessing, at the original use of each room, as – room after room – they passed through kitchen and larder, granary and stables, the immensely low, immensely long sheepfold, and then – just after – constructed one on top of another: winepress, distillery, and cellar. As always with agrarian architecture, only the smallest part of the farmhouse served human needs. And even then, such as in the small bedrooms upstairs, the walls had been pierced with deep pockets for supporting – eight weeks of the year – so many flat, cross-hatched lattices. On them, uninterruptedly, silkworms once fed.

It was coming out of the dark farmhouse, however, and into the bright sunlight beyond that Guy Fallows first spotted the *pigeonnier*. It stood in the far, south-east corner of the courtyard, forming in fact one of the courtyard's extremities. A few broken carts, coloured *bleu gauloise*, lay casually propped about its base. Their handles, straight as iris stalks, only added, it seemed, to the sheer thrust of the tower, its verticality. It didn't so much rise, however, as self-gather, self-accumulate – a perfect cylinder of carved stone – in a movement that Guy Fallows found both massive and immensely – inexplicably – weightless.

Intrigued and, perhaps, already moved, he walked towards it. The dovecote was built on two levels. Below, flush with the ground, a stout little door with a gothic arch led into what must have served, once, as a tool-shed, or chicken coop, or rabbit hutch. Another door, at the very head of a small, exterior staircase, and of the exact same dimensions, stood directly over it. Guy Fallows noted that – at that very level – the stones changed colour. They went from grey to blonde: from so many weather-worn, lichen-struck blocks to something pale, faintly golden, like bales of freshly shorn wheat. They did so without any apparent rupture. The tower went on climbing to form a single, harmonious mass, as if the entire structure had not only been conceived but executed in one effortless gesture.

'Quite something,' his son remarked, coming up from behind.

'Quite something,' Fallows agreed.

'Quite a surprise, too, don't you think?' the son asked. The two of them were standing about the base of the dovecote, staring up. A few clouds, blown by a light but persistent wind, made it appear as if the tower itself were moving – and briskly – across the radiant spring sky.

'Yes, quite a surprise, indeed,' Guy Fallows answered.

He had the impression, now, examining its girth, its successive ranks of perfectly matched, overlapping, limestone rectangles, that he wasn't so much *seeing* the stone tower, as *hearing* it. He was listening to the stones as if the stones, in their exquisite joinery, were sounds, and the sounds belonged to some piece of prose he'd always wished – and hopelessly failed – to have written.

Something, altogether, began to stir in Guy Fallows as he gazed at the dovecote. For if the stones 'spoke' to him, they addressed a part of his inner being he'd long since considered closed, as if sealed, impervious to everything but its own darkness. That part lay – he knew – like a hard, resilient core. A tumour. And – with each, succeeding year – had grown only darker, deafer, more malignant.

He needed to know more. Needed to know how something as seemingly incidental as an abandoned bit of rural architecture could 'speak', when virtually everything else in his own life had fallen into silence. He needed – first of

11

all – to return by himself. To bring pencils and notepaper, maybe even a tape-measure, and gather everything he could about those 'sounds'. Gather everything that lay, it seemed, in a resonant circle, about that whole, deserted work.

'Quite a surprise, quite a surprise,' his son kept repeating as the two of them, now, made their way home. On the narrow footpath back, Andrew Fallows was referring to nothing in particular except, perhaps, some abstract of his own making: of the afternoon, the air about them, and the dissolving (perhaps already dissolved) memory of the grey dovecote that went – at a certain height – straw blonde.

The very next morning, Fallows returned. All night he'd thought restlessly about the tower, about the *pigeonnier* without pigeons. Even in his sleeplessness, though, he hadn't so much seen as 'heard' it: 'heard' its illegible paragraphs, its mute chapters as if laid – in so many dense, hand-quarried blocks – into some totally transparent text. Yes, he was back, the next morning, and delighted to be so.

He took a whole series of notes, at first, on the facture of the work, on the material aspects of its execution. He measured, as well as he could, the dovecote's height and breadth, the circumference of the double belt-courses that ran – looped – about its entire girth. The lower of those two courses, with its delicately fluted gutter, was designed – he knew – to keep rodents from invading the dovecote proper, while the upper of the two served as a kind of circular esplanade upon which the pigeons might strut, or dry their plumage, or simply – as the English say – 'take the air'.

It was on entering the dovecote itself, however, that Fallows had his greatest surprise. He'd climbed the outer stairway, its steps worn smooth as marble and furrowed (both by rain and by sheer, human traffic) deep as the rockers on a child's cradle. Pushing the low, lead-panelled door open now, Fallows looked up. He found himself confronting not so much a structure destined for the specific purpose of bird husbandry, as the tiny, immensely compact interior of some miniature cathedral. For, lining the walls like the pipes of an organ, and rising, in even tiers, clear to the curve of the dome, stood the hand-carved pocket holes in which pigeons, once, had nested. Their droppings, in fact, a phosphorescent white, still streaked the masonry. Over this, as if sprouting from its raised piers, the domed ceiling – a *gloria* unto itself – hung like a floating hood. It lay braced by two, intersecting arches that – languorous as the petals of a lily – came to touch, and, in touching, to support a stout, octagonal keystone. Upon the keystone, in a somewhat rudimentary fashion, a heart had been carved.

Fallows noted all of this meticulously. And, as he did, he wondered whether what he'd 'heard' in all that keyed stonework hadn't, in reality, been music rather than language. He was enthralled. He spent the entire morning taking what he called 'measure' of the place, knowing that to interpret so much silent dictation, to learn what the stones – the stone-mason – had intended, required, first of all, a material appreciation of the work itself. And the work, he knew, was something considerable.

He looked upon it, that morning, as the ill might look on some reputedly miraculous source. For Guy Fallows, who'd come to question – question and doubt – every aspect of his own existence, the tower stood – in all its splendour and simplicity – as something not only resolved and entire, but, perhaps, redemptive as well.

'Stone by stone, syllable by syllable,' he scribbled into his pocket notebook by way of counsel. It marked, in reality, the very beginning – the first words, the first gesture on that very first morning – of his life's last engagement. Whatever remained of that life would be spent, now, on elucidating that 'silent dictation'.

3

'Come ahead, come ahead, by all means,' Maurice Daubigny exhorted over the telephone. 'Come around six, say, and we'll all have a pastis together.' He added that it wasn't he, though, whom Fallows should be asking about the *bastide*, that sprawling farmhouse on which – like a watchtower – the *pigeonnier* was situated, but his wife, Solange. 'It was hers, once, you understand, her family's. It's all gone now, of course, sold and resold, but come ahead, Fallows, yes, by all means. My wife knows the place like the palm of her hand. She grew up there, after all. Yes, say about six, that would be perfect. We'll be expecting you,' he said, then added, good-heartedly, 'So will the pastis.'

Each time Guy Fallows had met Maurice Daubigny (at parties, at the inauguration of someone's pool or someone else's paintings, or simply running into him in any of the village restaurants), Daubigny had infallibly asked – at the propitious moment – whether or not Guy Fallows hunted. Each time, his voice would go into a kind of hush. Then, he'd utter the self-same question between two rows of hopelessly neglected teeth. He'd do so as if venturing upon some ultimate form of intimacy: 'You don't hunt, by any chance, do you?'

To which Fallows, invariably, would answer, 'No, but I whistle.'

'Whistle?'

'Yes, walking through the woods. I whistle to keep hunters like yourself from mistaking me for a hare or a partridge. Or – even worse – some wild boar,' Fallows would say, smiling.

Daubigny hunted boar, exclusively boar, and was continuously organizing parties, even months before the season opened, out of some gleeful, monomaniac anticipation. He thought, in fact, of little else, not even the immense gravel pits near Orgon which he owned and offhandedly managed. He lived – all year long – for the first Sunday in September, and for as many bristling, wild pigs as he could bag in the brief, three-month season that followed. So Guy Fallows wasn't the least bit surprised, shaking hands with Daubigny that afternoon under the gracious portico of his Ménerbes manor house, to find him looking this way, then that. He was forever on the *qui-vive*, hoping to hear a single leaf rustle. To catch sight, perhaps, of the tip of some tall, hairy ear, twitching in the very midst of his own, heavily sprinkled rhododendrons.

Nor was Guy Fallows astonished, an instant later, when Daubigny leant towards him, and once again whispered, in that special hush of his, '*Tu ne chasses pas, par hasard?*'

'*Non, mais je siffle.*'

'Ah,' Daubigny exclaimed, 'I remember, now. Of course you don't. You're the American novelist who doesn't hunt. An anomaly, a pure anomaly,' he said in high spirits. 'Please, please come in.' Then added, 'You *do* drink pastis, though, don't you?'

Solange Daubigny was someone altogether different. A rather thin, elegant woman in her mid-40s, she was as outwardly cheerful, well disposed, even radiant, as she was (Fallows suspected) inwardly discontent. She hid this behind a faultless affability and, that afternoon, a shower – a burst foam, really – of infinitesimally small flowers, printed across her knee-high, high-collared silk dress. Forget-me-nots, Guy Fallows registered, half-consciously. It was her walk, though, and especially her posture, he noted, that revealed or, rather, suggested some second nature. For no matter how briskly, affirmatively she entered her own living room that very instant, there was something about her hips, and, perhaps, the cup of her shoulders that dragged reluctantly behind. That seemed to lag, sullenly. That didn't wish to enter either the room or that exchange of perfect banalities she was just – that very moment – exposing herself to.

Someone less perceptive than Fallows, perhaps, wouldn't have noticed a thing. She came across the highly polished tile floor now (the tiles themselves spread like a taut fishnet of lozenges, waxed to the lustre of water), her high heels clicking smartly as she came, and her small hand extended in greeting.

'We certainly have a lot to talk about,' she said convivially, 'what with our children leading the kind of life that they do.' Here, too, Fallows detected an undercurrent of hidden meanings, a cache of secrets. 'The kind of life' that his son, Andrew, and her daughter, Vic, shared together was, in fact, typical of their entire generation: they came and went as they chose, slept together as they pleased, and altogether thrived in a kind of fragile insouciance of their own. For whatever constraints they'd escaped, however, they had to confront a world – Guy Fallows well knew – that no social order could either prepare them for, nor protect them from. Their plight, he recognized, would be far the harder.

But he wasn't at the Daubignys' to talk about Andrew (Andrew's business, he felt, was entirely his own) nor to chatter about whatever small subjects they might possibly have in common. He was there for the tower. He was there for whatever scraps of private history, anecdote, even documentation he could gather. Because some time between the moment he'd first caught sight of the *pigeon-nier* and the instant he'd picked up the telephone and called Daubigny, the idea of writing a long piece, a story, a novel even, about that weightless work and its vanished artisan had simply gelled. Had taken on, in no time whatsoever, all the properties – the heightened significance – of an obsession. The story would be, Fallows had decided, the last chance – the very last chance – he'd give himself. In regard to that, at least, he was thoroughly resolved.

So, after the usual exchange of pleasantries, Fallows directed the conversation – bit by bit – towards the dovecote and its sprawling, rose-coloured farmhouse, the property once of Solange Daubigny, *née* St Chamas. It wasn't a subject, though, to interest her husband. He began, almost immediately, to fidget. It was far too far from that wilderness he doted on with its broken twigs and low, rushing husks. From those black, 140-kilo bundles of plunging meat. He poured himself another pastis, and, excusing himself, left the two of them – in their fanned, rattan armchairs – to discuss the vicissitudes of that lost estate.

And vicissitudes there were. For no sooner had Solange Daubigny sold the farmhouse in the mid-1970s – as she explained to Fallows – than prices began to soar. The Belgian couple who'd acquired it, sold it in turn for a tidy profit five years later. In fact, they doubled their original investment without having unblocked a gutter, cemented a stone, replaced a roof-tile. For the first two summers running, they'd camped like transients in the *bergerie*, then abandoned the place altogether: they'd found it 'much too primitive' for their tastes. The Swiss decorators who then purchased it had even less to do with the property. They'd come down Easters, and Easters only. With a whole band of friends, clients, investors, they'd check into a local five-star hotel, and there dress and disguise themselves 'rustic' for what had now become their annual saturnalia. By the light of the full moon and to the sounds of a six-piece orchestra that they'd have brought down from Berne and then concealed in what had once been the cocoonery, they'd cavort, chase one another naked through the open doors and broken gateways, couple in hay cut thirty years earlier and gone now, with so much steady desiccation, a furtive, indeterminate grey. Their cries – cries of joy, panic, and even, occasionally, pain – could be heard, on those moonlit nights, from kilometres away.

Worse, though, was yet to come. For the decorators, 'recognizing a good thing when they saw one', sold the whole estate in the late 1980s to a somewhat obscure bank on the outskirts of Zurich. The bank had been founded, funded, and had steadily prospered on the grounds of some highly delicate, highly dubious, legal nuance. In reality, the bank was nothing less than an elaborately disguised holding company, owned, in turn, by a vast Japanese consortium, based in Kyoto. The bank in Zurich, the consortium in Kyoto, had probably never seen – never needed to see – the farmhouse that it owned in Provence. Overrun with bramble and fig, and invaded each summer by whole armies of shrill, ventriloquial *cigales*, the farm would appear, in Kyoto, as nothing more than a brief listing on the flickering green screens of the consortium's computers. For there, it was nothing more than that: a minor investment in a vast portfolio of investments touching on nickel, sulphur, on paper mills and their subjacent publishing houses, on the reinvested profits of several so-called independent universities, on a castle here, a reputed vineyard there, and – scattered a bit everywhere – grocery chains, funeral parlours, beauty salons, three whole film studios: whatever they'd managed – bit by bit

18

– to bring into their control and add to the ever-growing inventory of their tentacular, worldwide cartel.

But it wasn't this that interested Guy Fallows. It wasn't *now* that mattered to him, but *then*. But that world that existed before its least living particle had been appraised, speculated upon, relegated to a scale of so many spurious digits. But *then, then*, Guy Fallows insisted. When the world was still rooted to something that resembled an earth. When whatever grew, grew through the toil and tending of human hands. When the work of those hands not only created but substantiated existence, and gave to the smallest thing its own, specific dignity. Yes, hands, fingers, Guy Fallows thought: thought of that very force that had quite literally scooped, drawn, raised that sprawling farmhouse, once, out of the obdurate earth. Had ploughed, stacked, laid its each and every field-stone; had hewn and sawn the wood for its doors and shutters and floorboards; had baked its tiles; hammered out its still-red hooks and door handles and harness chains. Hands, he thought, almost angrily. For then, he went on, everything that was was *touched*. Everything bore the invisible but unmistakable imprint of human labour, and created – out of that labour – perhaps as its most precious acquisition (more than its crops, than the ghostly slip of its white asparagus or so many cleaved melons, tumbling across the dark, storeroom floor), the notion of its own presence. Its own being. The earning of the word: *here*.

Instinctively, now, Guy Fallows glanced across at Solange Daubigny's hands. They were no longer those of a peasant's, certainly, but they retained – despite their slenderness – a deliberateness of movement and an economy of means that, for Fallows, bespoke their origin. At that very instant, in fact, they – Solange Daubigny's hands – were preparing Fallows a fresh pastis. While one hand grasped the handle of a squat, ceramic water pitcher, the other (by the very

19

tips of its fingers) held a tall glass tumbler. In it, several inches of that acid green *apéritif* sloshed idly about. As she filled it with cold water, though, the acid green turned – as if alchemized – into a milky cylinder of pale jade.

'How's that?' she asked.

'Perfect,' he replied, taking the drink. Doing so, he caught a distinct whiff of her perfume. Floral, diffuse, its bouquet of scents was dominated by that of honeysuckle. Fallows knew it well. In fact, sitting there, drink in hand, he felt the redolence of that scent invade every part of his being. In only an instant, it travelled across twenty years of memory, and entered – as it did – into his every pore, his every awakened cell. It both excited and disturbed him.

Now, as Solange Daubigny returned to her tall wicker chair, Fallows felt strangely deprived. He searched for that scent, once again – that aroma of wild honeysuckle – and found, suddenly, nothing. Suddenly, no one. Solange Daubigny had already taken her place, rather primly, in that tall wicker chair as if nothing had 'happened'. As if the lees of Guy Fallows's memory hadn't – an instant earlier – been stirred to the quick.

She'd begun telling him, in fact, the little she knew about the *pigeonnier*. 'There's so little to go on,' she said, sipping her drink. 'There are hardly any documents to speak of: only some tattered notarized deeds. Those, and whatever little scraps I can still recall from childhood. You know, the rumours, the hearsay, all the particular folklore that attaches itself to a place.'

It was certain, though – as she explained it – that the *pigeonnier* had been built several centuries prior to the farm. That, as opposed to the usual order of things, the farmhouse had sprouted up, had grown and flourished about its dovecote, rather than the opposite. 'It was the heart of the whole place,' Solange Daubigny explained. 'It drew us like a magnet. It was there, as children, that we went with our games, tried on our disguises, played out our very first fantasies. Where we hid when lightning struck, and later, much later, went to whisper to the stones what we wouldn't dare whisper to anyone – anything – else.'

Yes, just as Fallows had suspected, the tower had been constructed at two distinct periods. The original dovecote, built some time in the middle of the sixteenth century, had fallen almost totally into ruin, and been reconstructed – stone after fitted stone – as recently as the 1940s. In fact, as Solange Daubigny explained, it was in 1944, just prior to her own birth, that an obscure Italian mason began working alone with no more support than what his own muscle and skill would bring each day to the carving, keying and laying of those stones. There, bit by bit, he'd literally resurrected – as if he were dealing with light, or air, or some weightless liquid – the whole, dilapidated structure.

It would be the very first time that Guy Fallows would hear Guido Stampelli's name mentioned. It would be the very first time, as well, that the sound of those two names, of 'Guy' and 'Guido', would resound as derivatives, one of the other. As near-perfect homonyms. Unfortunately, though, Solange Daubigny could tell Fallows nearly nothing about Guido Stampelli himself.

'I know, though,' she suggested, 'a bit more – perhaps – than I should.'

'How do you mean?' he asked.

She hesitated a moment, drawing the gold thread of a hair free from that bed of minuscule blue flowers – forget-me-nots – that lay printed across her silk dress. 'You see,' she began, then hesitated once again. 'You must understand, first, that my mother was a deaf-mute. She never spoke. She gave signs, gestures, instead. When I was a bit older, she began writing me little notes, and we'd correspond – best as we could – sending those notes back

21

and forth. It was like a card game of our own. But we never really communicated in the usual sense of the word. We never conversed. With each passing year, though, I came to know what my mother meant, *really* meant, not merely from her messages – her little notes – but from her silences. From everything that she'd leave unsaid.'

Here, Solange Daubigny paused, took a long sip from her drink. Nervously, she ran a hand over the folds of her dress, drawing it smooth across the curve of her thigh. 'Whenever I'd ask her about the tower, you see, that silence would grow. She'd answer, of course. But she'd answer as if on either side of the question. She'd leave – in the very middle – a kind of void. A blankness. And that blankness, with each passing year, would grow only greater, blanker.

'So, I'd learn by omission. I'd come to realize exactly how important the *pigeonnier*, and Guido Stampelli who'd rebuilt the *pigeonnier*, must have been for my mother simply by the cloud that surrounded any mention of either. Nothing for a child, of course, could be more intriguing. But what – really – can I tell you? For I'd never learn, you see, what those silences actually contained. Something within them was too important, too dangerous, or simply too delicate to be mentioned. And words, written words, words written out on little scraps of paper and passed back and forth across a waxed coffee table, were being used to make certain that whatever it was, wasn't said. Wasn't even suggested.'

Solange Daubigny stood up and walked slowly towards the open window-doors. Once again, Guy Fallows detected that slight reluctance in the way she carried herself: something in the roll, perhaps, of her hip bone, he speculated. Just beyond the open window-doors, the tiered leaves of an immense chestnut tree lay splashed in sunlight.

'As for my father,' she said, staring out on to the leaves,

22

'that's altogether a different matter. With my father, you see,' her blonde hair catching, that very moment, in the bright sunlight, 'I only wish I knew less. I could go on forgetting everything I know about my father for the rest of my life, and would still wish I knew less.' She stood there, somewhat rigidly, staring out. 'Less and less,' she continued, her voice tapering now to a mere thread, to a thin trickle of sound. Gradually, she seemed to forget Fallows's presence altogether. She'd begun talking to no one, perhaps, but the leaves beyond, of that unexpungeable memory of a father for whom there seemed – indeed – to be too much, rather than too little, to speak of.

Her bright hair flashed green in the light that rose and fell – like paddled water – off those long, breeze-rustled leaves. While Fallows listened, she stood there staring out, murmuring now, almost inaudibly, to no one if not to the leaves themselves.

In the weeks that preceded the very first lines of Guy Fallows's last novel, he gathered whatever he could. From those in the village and surrounding countryside, as well as from Solange Daubigny herself, he took careful note of anything touching upon Guido Stampelli and that seemingly weightless *pigeonnier* he'd constructed, or rather reconstructed, nearly half a century earlier. Fallows harvested every rumour he could concerning that period, and the small cast of characters of which it was composed. As for Emmanuel St Chamas, Solange's father, Fallows didn't need to search far. His was a story that everyone knew. His was the story, indeed, that his own daughter had never been able to forget. It didn't so much touch upon the life of Emmanuel St Chamas *per se*, as upon one particular, ineffaceable night of that life in mid-August, 1944. That night, a small band of adolescents, carrying everything from their fathers' shotguns to pitchforks and switchblades, and riding the back of a small lorry that they'd 'borrowed' for the occasion, fell into an ambush and were slaughtered by the very Nazis that – in full retreat – they'd come down out of their terraced hillsides and olive groves and rabbit hutches to cut short, and execute, themselves.

Only St Chamas could have denounced them. Aside from the boys' own fathers and immediate families, only he was in a position to 'get wind' of their plans. His farmhouse was simply too close to theirs. Furthermore, his sympathies were a secret to no one: he'd collaborated with the occupying armies from the very first day of their arrival.

When, early the next morning, the Resistance came to settle accounts, St Chamas wasn't to be found in his sprawling farmhouse but hidden in the tiny, candle-lit crypt of the church at Notre-Dame des Lumières. He wasn't alone, either. Clustered around him in a tight circle, four or five priests, facing outwards and holding each other's hands across their crossed arms, had formed a kind of *cordon ecclésiastique*. They were praying. While their black robes hung to the stone floor, their eyes rolled up in supplication towards the low, overhanging vault of the crypt. The heavy rush of their 'Hail Marys' reverberated against those walls – that vault – like so many amplified heartbeats. Like waves, too, bursting inside their rock grottoes.

All the while, St Chamas stood cowering in the midst of that narrow circle that the priests – hand in hand – had created for his protection. While his fate, quite literally, was being decided, he stared fixedly down at his tall, mud-caked boots. He himself was praying to no one if not his own, all-but-extinguished star.

Somehow the priests, that morning, managed to dissuade the *maquisards* from executing their guest, as they called him. The priests did so more out of the magic that was still – vestigially – attached to their office than out of any reasoned argument. Next day, St Chamas was smuggled not only out of the crypt, the church, and the township itself, but out of the very country. He'd spend the next two years of his life, safely hidden, in a mission that the priests maintained somewhere in the very heart of the Cameroons. There, he'd be protected, as a would-be saint might, from those who'd tear him apart – if they could – for the sake of his bones. Reduce him – if they could – to his least splinter.

4

'Honeysuckle,' Guy Fallows murmured to himself, driving home. How much easier it is, he thought, to retain the sound of that flower than its scent. To hear, over and over, the lilt of its 'honey' get swallowed – glottal – by the heavy consonants of its 'suckle'.

But the scent, the scent vanishes, he thought. Vaporizes. Hadn't it been over twenty years, now, since he'd smelt it on another living creature? Since he'd held her – the very first time – in the darkness of a barn so dark they seemed but voices. Voices, and the vaguest outlines of each other's body. Yes, and then, suddenly, that scent, that redolence, that unmistakable signature. He'd held her so gently, at first, that it felt as if he were holding – in his arms – a whole shrub of honeysuckle. A bush, the full height of a human. As he pressed her closer, though, she grew not brittle, like a bush, but full. The closer he pressed her, in effect, the fuller she grew. And the more pungent the odour of that wild, thicket flower became.

It was the beginning of the happiest years of his life. They'd be short-lived, but would possess an intensity such as he'd never known before. Nor – he quickly added – known since. It was an intensity based as much on each other's separate productivity as on their own, mutual enthralment. One fed the other. For both of them, in their early twenties, were creators: he, of course, as a young, aspiring novelist. And she, as a clay sculptor, already recognized in her native Finland as a 'child prodigy'.

Then, too, they both shared a common and profound love of Provence, that land of their predilection. 'What first brought you here?' he asked her, just after they'd met.

'The earth,' she answered.

Fallows, naturally enough, took this to mean the vineyards and terraced orchards of that rich yet arduous country. To mean the parched heath, aflame – at that time of year – with so much fan-tailed broom. To suggest the dark gullies of the Luberon, rich in crickets and in the needlework of their blue, iridescent dragonflies. Yes, earth indeed, he thought.

Fallows, just as easily, might have answered 'air', if she'd asked the same question. Answered, air and the thirty-two winds of Provence. Answered, a certain kind of inner respiration that he'd fled America – in those culturally stifling years – to discover. But she didn't ask. Discreet, and every bit as protective of his privacy as of her own, she rarely asked – in fact – any questions whatsoever. She would have considered them – in the light of her own, near-painful sensitivity – as intrusions.

It took him months, in effect, to realize that what she'd meant by 'earth' wasn't the land they lived in, but literally soil, and most particularly a certain red clay she employed in her own sculpture. She'd found a vein of that clay somewhere near Gargas (where, exactly, she'd never tell), and would return with so many still wet buckets of the stuff, malleable as some living organ, in the back of their bouncing, second-hand Deux-chevaux.

Within days, that damp clay would have been shaped into torsos, heads, entire bas-reliefs of figures picking clay apples off the clay branches of a windblown orchard, composed exclusively of that self-same material. Then,

27

turbaned in rags, the figures would await firing. On tall stools and trestle-tables, they'd stand – like souls awaiting judgment – before that weekly flame. There, once and for all, they'd take on their fixed and immutable form, their blind gazes baked, pale vermilion.

Hands, once again, Guy Fallows reflected. For everything the two of them did, in those years, they did with their hands. Be it her highly accomplished terracotta figures, or his own meticulous paragraphs (worked virtually to the knuckle by one lead pencil after another), it was the hands – the working fingers – that did them. And living, in those years, in a quiet, unspoken symbiosis with farmers (who still considered themselves – with a certain pride – as *paysans*), they knew that it was this alone that gave dignity to their lives. Whether it be the hands that held the braces for the heavy, late autumn ploughing, or those – infinitely more delicate – that traced the curve of a particular hip in wet clay, it was this – these, once again – that, yes, gave meaning to all else.

What's more, life then was not only simple, tactile, immediate, but astonishingly inexpensive. For next to nothing, they could feed themselves: for ten francs, buy a whole basketful of fresh fruit and vegetables, a shoulder of lamb, and those soft, flat, moon-white goats' cheeses they'd spread across so much still warm *pain complet*. They could buy wine, pumped through a hose pipe, for a franc a litre, and locally pressed olive oil for little more. Eventually, they'd even manage to purchase a little house for themselves with a good-sized barn, alongside. Bit by bit, they'd convert the barn into a studio. But best – best of all – the relative ease of their lives gave them time. Time to develop their own, particular vision of things. And time to acquire the skills – the necessary techniques – for expressing that vision. Never would there be such promise to their lives. Such joy.

'It's all here, isn't it?' she said, looking out on to the far fields. The fields had gone violet – at that hour – in the shadows cast by the last of the sun.

'Yes,' Fallows said, and then, taking her in his arms, 'And here, here, too.'

'Oh yes, here, here, so very much here,' she replied, as he drew her gently down on to the ground, and felt – once again – as if he were entering a bush – a whole arbour – of honeysuckle. 'Yes, yes,' she said, as the scent grew stronger and stronger – it seemed – with each thrust. With their own, steadily gathering rhythm. 'Yes, just here,' she added. 'Just exactly here.'

It lasted no more than three years, and ended – before it ended – on the very morning she realized she was pregnant. She didn't tell Fallows, at first. Didn't want to speak of it, even to herself. But, within days, he realized that something – clearly – had gone wrong. She left signs of it, everywhere. She'd stopped cleaning her sculpting tools, for instance, at the end of each afternoon: those impeccably kept wire-loops and spatulae. And – what might have amounted to the very same thing – stopped washing, twice daily, as she always had. In short, she began letting herself go. Her work, her appearance, the buoyant lustre of her brown gaze as it once alighted upon a flower, or a poised insect (while the tips of her fingers already seemed to be shaping those forms to those in her imagination), had begun undergoing a terrible change.

Of all the signs, however, the very first that Fallows remarked was – indeed – the honeysuckle. She'd stopped wearing it, altogether. From one day to the next, it had simply vanished. Vanished for ever.

She didn't want the baby. Nor could she bring herself to abort. She was far too close to nature – its ways – to consider such a choice. There was a third alternative,

29

however, and she took it. Gradually, she began abusing herself. Like all genuinely creative people, she had her dark, destructive side. And – bit by bit, day after day, more and more – this darkness manifested itself. After the second month of her pregnancy, she stopped sculpting altogether, and began drinking. Drinking that all too available, all too inexpensive hose-pipe wine from the local *cave coopérative*. Drinking, first at home, in her now abandoned studio. Then, soon after, drinking in the cafés as well. Drinking in the village cafés with whomever she knew, or happened to meet. Whomever – glass after glass – could keep pace.

Later, Fallows would date his own acute problems with alcohol to that very period. Loving his wife as he did, he'd wanted to 'stay with her' at any cost. He'd follow her to the cafés, drink as much as she would. And, like her, let his work slip, then fade: that first, ongoing wave of pure inspiration. It would never return. He'd never again create with such ease, such fluency of style. Never again translate – so readily – experience into so much articulated prose as he did during those first, crucial years. Nor, he added, ever again know such happiness.

The only children she wished to bear, he well understood, were her own earthen images: those tall, terracotta figures she crafted with such skill. She'd had a deeply disturbed childhood herself, and perhaps – at some hidden level – couldn't support the idea that it might be repeated. So, instead, she gave birth to those baked forms. Swaddled in so much inanimate mud, they – at least – would never know anguish. Never know fright.

Drunk much of the time, now, and still hiding from her own swollen belly, she nonetheless gave birth – on the last day of June – to Andrew Fallows. Then, just two weeks after, vanished. Abandoned both her newborn baby and her husband, and disappeared altogether.

On that very day, she left all her unfired sculptures standing out in a heavy downpour. When Guy Fallows discovered them, their features had all but washed away. They stood there – in the rain – smooth as socks. As faces in a smudged photograph. Having no eyes, now, they gazed at perfectly nothing. About the base of each, a small puddle of clay had already begun gathering.

Twenty years, he thought. They'd accumulated like so much weight, pulling him with each year – with each 'nearly effective', 'still somewhat wanting' novel – downward. No, he hadn't failed exactly. But he hadn't succeeded, either. And, with time, the immense promise of those early years – that *âge d'or* they'd shared together – had turned into a kind of dark ballast. Ponderous, consumptive, it had – bit by bit – drawn Fallows under. Had driven him to consider, in fact – for whole periods at a time – his own end.

Happily, though, he'd had his son to look after. Andrew, whom he loved, and had cared for – through the years – whole-heartedly. Often, indeed, this relationship had provided Fallows with his sole *modus vivendi*. His only veritable purpose. It didn't, however, keep that 'weight', that 'dark ballast', from continuing to gather, year after year. Yes, with each relative failure, each concomitant breakdown in self-esteem, he was drawn under that much deeper. Sometimes, in fact, he'd even *felt* its oppressiveness. *Felt* it falling like a kind of ash. Like some acid rain. *Felt* it gather, not about, but within him.

Twenty years, he went on thinking. He was seated, just then, at his desk, facing the late afternoon landscape, beyond. Once again, those very same violet shadows had as if underlined each and every vine-row. He sat there, a bottle of that local, hosepipe wine standing, as always, alongside his blank notepad, and remembered.

31

Remembered her. Remembered then. Yes, twenty years, he reflected. But he might just as well have murmured forty. Yes, forty years, already. Might just as well have returned to that incident, that story that hid (as did every story, he felt convinced) behind its own foil. Yes, might have sat there recalling that very day – very moment – in which he'd learn of his father's death. Would overhear, as a child, how his father had leapt – yes, plummeted – from the fifteenth floor of an office building to the city pavement, below.

'Dark ballast', indeed. Hadn't his whole life, in fact, been but a singleminded struggle to surmount that very moment? That fall he was never meant to know of?

With adolescence, Guy Fallows would gradually discover language. Its power of response. Would come – bit by bit – to recognize in words an autonomy of their own. For words, as he observed, rose. Were alleviative. Where everything else in his life had fallen, words, phrases, whole paragraphs – if properly executed – seemed to float, for Guy Fallows, with a buoyancy quite unlike anything else. Indeed, several years later, when the two of them met in Provence – her 'earth', his 'air' – the words as if pinnacled. Reached a height such as he never thought existed.

Perhaps, he reflected, it's just this, this weightlessness, that drew him, now, so powerfully towards the dovecote. For the tower reminded him of something he'd always – however obscurely – wished to emulate. Substantiate. Yes, it's 'silent dictation'. For stone after stone, it rose very much like the book he'd never written. Effortlessly, it seemed to project, as it climbed, its own affirmation: what Fallows, in that *âge d'or*, had once aspired to.

He'd gone back to the dovecote, now, three times. With each visit, his measure of the place had grown increasingly accurate. And, along with this, his sheer fascination. Gathering whatever he could concerning the *pigeonnier*, he'd also gone, periodically, to the village. There, he'd played *belote* with the old people, some of whom still remembered Guido Stampelli himself. Some, actually, could still recount – through their fading memory – vivid anecdotes.

Stones, he mused. Honeysuckle and stones. Just as soon as he'd put those two words together – heard them as if fit like jointed pieces – he felt something in his own heart as if coincide, as well. That afternoon, in fact, towards nightfall, he began.

5

*S*preading *the note open with his thumb, he read it as much with his moving lips as with his eyes. 'Propose,' he read, over and over, with that slow, laborious deliberation, attempting to extract the true sense of the word out of the morsels of its muttered sound. 'What do you propose?' she'd written.*

He stood in the very centre of that sombre living room, his cap in one hand, her note, now, in another, and faced her, seated across from him in a wide, upholstered armchair. It was late summer, and the high, electric buzzing of the cicadas outside had invaded the heavily shuttered room like so many dark sparks, or the tips of so much jangling wire. He'd even come to imagine, standing there, that in some covert manner, she commanded them, as well. Yes, he thought, even them. That as patrona, *there was nothing on her estate, no, not even the cicadas, that hadn't fallen totally under her control, and come to serve her interests, or at least her fancy, in one manner or another. He'd worked there, now, for six months. Worked for him, that is, rather than* her, *but hadn't – for a single instant – doubted 'who' was deciding 'what'. She reigned over those 300 hectares of richly cultivated earth with every bit as much acquired authority as inherent, incurable muteness.*

'Propose, what do you propose?'

He looked down at the crisp, unfolded square of note-paper, his thumb as if stamped at its base, the baked, undifferentiated colour of potato skin, and reread for the third time the question he knew he could never answer. Propose? Propose what? What – given his circumstances – did he have to propose? During those six months in which he'd been employed by Emmanuel St Chamas, he'd managed to clear the rubble free of the dovecote, recuperate whatever stones he could, and undertake – finally – the tower's reconstruction. In fact, he'd already laid in place, now, five courses of those stone blocks, which – at twenty-five centimetres a stone – amounted to a height of well over a metre of completed masonry. The tower, that is, had begun to rise. What more could she want? The work had proceeded roughly on schedule, and exactly as agreed upon. It had begun, as he called it, to leaven. What, then, was she asking?

At that very moment, she picked up her fountain pen and began scratching out a second note. He followed – upside down – the long, formal loops she was inscribing on that square block of blue notepaper. The block lay against her dress, balanced somewhere between her right thigh and kneecap. His thoughts, for an instant, lingered on or just beneath the dress's thick, earth-brown taffeta, imagining the slow curve of her thigh, the slight pommel of her knee-cap. He was, from time to time, as if invaded by thoughts – 'pictures', he called them – such as these. Despite his deep reserve, he'd let them happen. Let them flood his mind with those brief but vivid films of his patrona in various states of exposure. But he'd never – not even in his most unbridled fantasies – imagined her thoroughly naked. He'd always stopped short. Much as he might have wished otherwise, she preserved – yes, even in his wildest daydreams – a perfect inflexibility. An inviolacy born, no doubt, of unquestioned, unquestionable privilege.

That very instant, she handed him her second message. He walked halfway across the dark living-room floor, took it, then returned to that very same, self-designated square of red floor-tiles. He stood there, now, as if held to the unspoken rules of some unmentioned ceremony. With the double stumps of his short trousers round as cypress trunks and blue as so much wind-washed air, he stood there, and read. 'Propose,' it said. 'What do you propose,' it insisted, 'in lieu of payment? There's nothing left to pay you with, do you understand? What do you propose? This is a question. Answer it.'

So, he thought, it was *true. Everything he'd heard about the conditions under which St Chamas had been smuggled out of France and into Africa, weeks earlier, had turned out to be absolutely accurate. The entire countryside was talking about nothing else. For not only had St Chamas saved his own hide, and saved it* in extremis, *he'd even managed to escape with the entire contents of a joint, and now depleted, bank account. Marguerite St Chamas, for all her many hectares, had been left – in the midst of a war – penniless.*

Propose, propose, she'd written. For no matter how penniless she'd been left, there's nothing – he thought – that's going to stop her, stop them, stop any of those who employ the rest of us for their own purposes. For it's their world, he knew, not ours. It's ours to drain and plough, plant and harvest, to hack, rasp, and align, but it's theirs to possess. And nothing, not even a war, an armed occupation, will keep them from those steady, uninterrupted acts of acquisition. Stone after stone, crop after crop, season after season: nothing, absolutely nothing. Not even some base act of betrayal between spouses – of one spouse absconding with the funds of the other – nothing, according to Guido Stampelli, could disturb what he'd come to call, since adolescence, 'the order of things'.

Propose. Propose, indeed. But what, he asked himself. What did an immigrant stone-mason, living off the pickings of his own vegetable garden, and whatever meat (mostly rabbit) he could snare in his traps, have to propose?

'Sundays,' he suggested, breaking suddenly into that silence that hung over the room like mist over a vineyard, or a veil of smoke, floating – shroud-like – over so many freshly lit tapers. 'I could come Sundays, madame,' he continued, directing his words toward her eyes, talking not to be heard but to be seen. 'I could work on the pigeonnier in whatever spare time I have,' he suggested. 'That's what I could do. But I certainly wouldn't leave you like this.'

She scribbled out another note, quickly as she could. 'You won't,' it read. 'You won't leave me like this.'

She was watching his every word now, lip-reading not only what, but how he said it, detecting – from sight alone – that peasant diction he employed with all its marked, Piedmontese flourishes. 'You won't,' he read, over and over, standing there in the middle of Marguerite St Chamas's living room, his cap still held in one hand, and her note, pinched, in the other.

'But the stones,' he ventured. 'Who'll pay the quarry for the cost of the stones?'

'You will,' she quickly scribbled.

'And their transport? They cost just as much to carry down as they do to quarry. Who'll pay for that?'

Without a second's hesitation, she stretched her arm out – ruler-straight – in Guido Stampelli's direction. For an instant, he didn't quite understand what she meant by that abrupt gesture. Then, noticing that the index finger of her small, somewhat plump hand was pointed precisely in the direction of the last note she'd written, and that that note was still pinched firmly between his own thumb and forefinger, he stepped forward and surrendered it, if not to

37

Marguerite St Chamas, at least to her beckoning hand. No sooner had he done so, however, than she took the note, and – in a gesture of inveterate thrift – folded it back into that original square, its four angles immaculately matched. Then, once again, holding her arm out – ruler-straight – she handed Guido Stampelli, on that self-same piece of blue notepaper, her self-same response: 'You will,' it said.

'You will,' he read, over and over. But how, how, he kept asking himself. 'How?' he said, letting the word slip, inadvertently, from his thoughts to form, on his lips, the momentary emblem – the legible seal – of its very sound.

'However you see fit,' she scribbled back. 'There's always a means. Find it,' she wrote, underlining the words 'Find it' with two, sabre-like strokes.

He read and reread her brief, imperious message, furious not so much at her outrageous demands as by his own inability to meet them. For how, he asked himself, could he continue building the tower without any remuneration whatsoever, and still earn enough (even just enough) elsewhere to assure his own, basic needs? It was impossible, he knew. Even working the rest of the week for whatever clients he might, he'd still never make enough to pay for both the stones and their transportation; never compensate – not even with a full week's earnings – for each Sunday's expenses. Not to mention, he might have added, meeting his own monthly rent, and keeping himself in bread and wine, in lard, kerosene and matches: the basic necessities, that is, of his very existence. No, it was impossible, he realized. Utterly impossible.

But Marguerite St Chamas must have known more about Guido Stampelli, or more simply about men, than they did themselves. For at that very moment, that very instant within which her own, most vital interests seemed to waver in the balance (wouldn't she, some time later, claim that she'd never rest in her grave until the pigeonnier had been completed), she stood up and walked slowly towards a tall, oval, oak-framed mirror. A bit shorter than Guido usually imagined her, and quite a bit more buxom as well, she stood, back turned, so that her heavily lidded eyes and her small, pursed, heart-shaped mouth were discernible, now, only within the mirror's unwavering reflection. Her timing — under the circumstances — was faultless. So, too, was her choice of décor: that dark oval in which her own features would serve as unique attraction. For, at that very instant, her hands rose slowly up over her shoulders and behind her neck, and there — still rising — as if unleashed like ten, ferreting truffle dogs, ten, plump, burrowing fingers into the rich undergrowth of her high, piled, ruthlessly upswept hair. Unfastened, the pins swiftly recuperated within the palm of each hand, her hair came tumbling down. It tumbled in several, successive lengths, lapping over itself as it did, spreading as it fell. Guido Stampelli — at that exact moment — could have sworn that it resounded. Thundered. That something, at least, thundered as the hair fell in a slow waterfall to well below the line of Marguerite St Chamas's waist. There, the thunder as if stopped as the hair came gradually to settle in so many swirling pools — deep eddies — of a rich, almost rusting shade of Titian red.

Stock-still, Guido Stampelli looked on. His cap still fixed rigidly in one hand, her note in the other, he stared — terrified — into this living spectacle as if he himself had just transgressed some basic tenet of existence. Had just broken some covenant touching upon the essence itself of human comportment. Try as hard as he might, he couldn't justify his presence in that heavily shuttered room. Couldn't feel anything but wrong — indecent — witnessing the lavish unravelling of Marguerite St Chamas's hair. He hadn't the right, he well knew, to such things. Other women, yes.

Women whom he'd known, and worked with, and who, at day's end, were every bit as exhausted as himself. But this, but her, but the hair of the proprietor of so many floating hectares of fruit trees and rich, pampered, perfectly aligned vine-stalks; the hair that, covertly, held the deeds to all that pasture, all those flourishing expanses of oats and barley and sainfoin. That owned horses, and a forge of its own. The hair that had a perfect allée of mulberries leading to its door, and, beneath the mulberries, at least a hundred metres of violet iris, either side, standing stiffly at attention. To this, this head of hair, he knew, he had absolutely no rights whatsoever.

And rights he hadn't. For just then, Marguerite St Chamas, rather than reaching for a brush, or some heavy, tortoiseshell comb, and grooming that vast, deployed treasure of hers, set to gathering it, once again, into a single, uplifted mass. She did so nimbly, almost mechanically. With her left hand, she held her hair raised into place. With her right, she pulled hairpins from between her lips and stuck them – one after another – into that immense nest that Guido Stampelli could consider, now, only as some ultimate form of mystery.

The whole performance had taken no time whatsoever. The hair flaunted, exhibited really – an organ unto itself – had served its purpose. Far more than any overtly erotic demonstration (than a breast, say, poured with all its tiny quivers from the net of some unsnapped brassière), Marguerite St Chamas's unloosened bundle of red hair had filled Guido's mind with the demon of irresistibility. For – from that instant forth – the demon itself would permeate his thoughts, his feelings; would determine his each and every decision. From that instant forth, to whatever demand Marguerite St Chamas might make, Guido Stampelli would only be able to respond with an invariable – an unequivocal – 'yes'.

The first and most exacting of her demands followed almost immediately after. She'd just returned from that brief but luminous appearance in her very own mirror, her petticoat rustling like the sound of a small wood-fire as she came across the dark, living-room floor. Once settled, however, in her tall armchair, that sound gave way to the ambient silence, and, within that silence, to the scratching of a brass nib across a block of blue notepaper. The scratching in itself sounded more like the gnawing of some indefatigable rodent, hard at work in its larder. In the first of several messages, she wrote: 'Once the pigeonnier is completed, if I'm not mistaken, there'll be thirty courses (rangées) of carved stone, altogether, isn't that correct?'

Guido read the message, then nodded. 'Each of those courses is comprised, is it not, of forty-eight finished stones? What you receive, rough hewn, from the quarry, and then carve – fit into place – at the worksite (le chantier) itself? Isn't this the procedure? Isn't this what you do?'

Once again, Guido Stampelli nodded. He'd crossed over, taken the message from the pinched fingers of her plump, outstretched hand, then returned to the floor's very centre, motivated – all the while – by that self-same, unequivocal obedience. There, once again, standing in that identical, self-designated square of red floor-tiles, he'd opened out Marguerite St Chamas's message. Its little blue square seemed to sprout from his thumb into a delicate flora of lines, loops, dashes. Standing there solid, and – at the same time – thoroughly exposed, vulnerable, feeling the force of her presence invade every part of his being, he nodded, now, not so much at Marguerite St Chamas as at the black satin tip of her protruding shoe.

Her next message was executed in one, ruthless stroke. And – once again – he entered into that narrow ritual which brought him forwards as far as her outstretched arm, then back to that same, rigid patch of tiled flooring.

41

'Continuez,' *the message read, quite simply, and nothing more.*

'Continuez,' *Guido Stampelli read and reread, dumb to all else and standing – as if struck – at the very heart of that dark room, its tall shutters hooked fast against the low, late afternoon light. Continue, but how, he kept asking himself. How could he go on building – rebuilding – that broken* stone *pigeonnier without those small, indispensable sums, those tight increments of cash that – week after week, month after month – he somehow managed to live on? How could he possibly accept? How, though, he added (and in the very same breath), could he possibly refuse?*

At that very instant, the tip of Marguerite St Chamas's black satin shoe rose no more than two – perhaps three – centimetres from the angle it habitually rested at, and pointed in exactly the direction of Guido Stampelli's mid-section. The tip had stiffened like a member, or like an arrow – taut on its strung bow – and was directed, now, towards the very core of its living target.

Guido Stampelli felt struck by this infinitesimal adjustment. By the tiny, clandestine signal it emitted. Instinctively, his muscles tightened as if to receive the full thrust of what was still only imminent, impending, promised.

With the angle of that black satin toe held raised in place, Marguerite St Chamas wrote out the last of her messages. It was lengthy. It took several minutes to complete and covered five, separate sheets of that pale, cornflower-blue notepaper that, normally, she used so sparingly. Once finished, she folded each of the five sheets over, once, then twice. Pinched now between her thumb and forefinger, the whole message looked more like some tiny, toy accordion. She held it out in Guido Stampelli's direction, and waited for him to take it.

But he didn't. Or, rather, he couldn't. He couldn't move. He stood there as if paralysed by that pointed

*shoe, by the black ray that seemed to emanate from its
very tip, holding him like a votary within its power. Then
slowly, deliberately, calculating each centimetre as she
went, Marguerite St Chamas relaxed the tension that ran
from her ankle forward, thereby lowering the inflexion of
her entire foot, and – in so doing – freeing Guido Stampelli
from that narrow, hallucinatory siege.*

*'Continue,' the message read. 'I want you to continue,
do you understand? You've accepted this commission.
You've already committed yourself (vous vous êtes déjà
engagé). So continue, be equal (soyez égal) – I insist – to
your engagements,' the first of the five sheets read.*

*'It's my responsibility, in fact,' the second began, 'to see
that you do. To see that nothing keeps the* pigeonnier *from
completion. I'll be watching you, too, don't think that I
won't. From my bedroom window, I'll be keeping an eye
(je veillerai) on every move that you make, you can rest
assured,' the second note concluded.*

*'Forty-eight stones, you say, to a single row?' began the
third. 'At the completion of every row, if every stone in
that row has been properly measured, carved, laid into
place, I'll be offering you, as your compensation (votre
récompense), a little key with a green ribbon attached
to it, do you understand? I'll be leaving it just beneath
the . . .*

*'. . . beneath the stone trough,' the fourth note resumed.
'You know it, it's right alongside the stable doors, and filled
with flowering hollyhocks, right now. You'll find the key
just beneath it. Just under. But only on those days – at the
end of those days – in which you've completed an entire
row, do you understand? In the meanwhile (en attendant),
this offer should keep you busy (à l'oeuvre). Should keep
your mind upon the work.*

*'But a full circle, is that understood? A full circle of
masonry,' the fifth sheet concluded, 'before you receive*

43

the key. And washed, *as well, do you understand? You won't enter my bedroom, I insist, until you've thoroughly washed. Returned to your own house, and scrubbed yourself clean. Until you've shaved and put on fresh clothes and a starched collar, and smell of something other than a day labourer,* vous m'entendez?'

At that very moment, Marguerite St Chamas began running her naked hands up and down over the taffeta sleeves of her dress in a frenetic imitation of someone bathing. She pretended, now, to be scrubbing her shoulders, or drawing deep circles into the hollow of each cheek. She wouldn't stop, either. Guido Stampelli watched the terrible dance of those hands as they palpitated – just like two butterflies, he thought – over the surface of her body, alighting here, arising there, equivocating a bit everywhere.

He'd retain that image of her, in fact, for several days. 'Washed,' she'd written. And, in illustrating that single, unspoken command, the plump regent herself had entered into a wild, unbroken pantomime. Had surrounded herself in so much sterile gesture. With her dry, soapless hands, had wreathed her entire figure in the invisible gauze of an all too apparent hysteria.

It was the baker – well before dawn – who first heard it. He heard it at least three full minutes before he actually saw it: heard the heavy thumping of a charged wheelbarrow coming down over the humpbacked cobbles before he could actually recognize – in the light breaking like burst straw from his boulangerie door – Guido Stampelli, or at least Guido Stampelli's silhouette, directing the overloaded wheelbarrow as if drunkenly down the village street. The baker, out of simple discretion, returned to his work. He pretended to let Guido pass unnoticed. He checked his pocketwatch, however, hanging shiny from a nail against

44

the soot-dark, bakery wall. It was scarcely five in the morning.

'Paure colhon,' *he muttered to himself in a tone made up as much of pity as simple derision.* 'Poor bastard,' *he said. For Guido had taken to rising – now – at three each morning, and making his way to the quarry by any light available: moonlight, lamplight, or simply the afterglow – along the now abandoned service roads – of so much impacted, limestone dust. Once there, he'd climb into a niche: a kind of rock cubicle that the foreman had designated. Within it, he was free to carve – at half the going price – as much stone as he needed. By the light of whatever candles he'd brought in his stiff, canvas satchel, he'd begin sawing long, faultless, die-straight rectangles. He'd do so with the candlelight lapping the white flanks of his limestone cell on every side, and casting – as it did – a kind of frieze: a relief of shadows about the square-shaped scorings, high overhead.*

Guido Stampelli would work without stopping. He'd calculated, from the very first day (or, rather, the very first night), that in an hour and a half of continuous sawing, he could extract two, perfectly shaped rectangles. Two, that is, of the forty-eight that he'd need to complete a row – a course – about the dovecote's girth. By working quickly as well as carefully, he could not only manage to extract the stones well before dawn, each day, but transport them in his wheelbarrow, two at a time, delivering them – still before dawn – to the pigeonnier *itself, five kilometres away.*

This, then, is what the baker heard. Heard the thumping of Guido's wheelbarrow over cobbles, and – at the same time – that somewhat deaf knocking of one, matched, limestone block against another. This, too, would be what the entire village, and soon the entire countryside, would hear, or – rather – hear of, hear spoken: that Guido

45

Stampelli was working overtime, and at bizarre hours, for that thoroughly detested landowner, Marguerite St Chamas. That probably he was doing so for nearly no wages whatsoever. (Hadn't others, before him? Weren't there rumours to that effect?) That 'aquela salòpa', as they called her, had had him on. And that, for her vicious little favours, he was ready to rise at three o'clock each morning, and not only haul the stones that he'd just hand-sawn off the walls of the quarry, carting them all those kilometres to that sprawling farmhouse, but lay them as well. Lay them two at a time, and before the sun had even started to rise. Before, that is, Guido's normal workday had even commenced.

But why, they wondered. For what? For pleasuring in the buttocks of the wife of the land's arch-collaborator? For the taste of so many tart, fascist kisses? The rumours, and − along with the rumours − the insults, half scathing, half commiserating, grew more and more rampant from week to week. But if Guido heard any of it, he didn't seem to notice. He moved through the whispers, the glances, the sudden, conspiratorial density that seemed to gather, now, about any group, with all the indifference of someone hiking in high boots through so much stunted bramble. If, indeed, he noticed it at all, he didn't seem to care. Guido had already undergone his conversion.

Now, he'd just arrived. He finished unloading the two matching, limestone blocks, almost pouring them − one at a time − out of the wheelbarrow and on to a tattered horse blanket he kept for exactly such operations. He dragged the blanket, now, with its ungainly charge until it was nearly flush with the dovecote proper. From there, he could just manage to hoist the 52-kilo blocks on to the makeshift scaffold, overhead. The boards of the scaffold (as white from stone dust as from so much sloshed, overturned mortar) bent deeply now as Guido added his own weight to that of the blocks, and brought himself up, hauling the satchel – clattering with tools – after him. Yes, now indeed he was there. And no sooner had he levered the stones into place (lifting them – that is – off the boards and on to the masonry itself, so that they stood, now, at shoulder height) than he looked out over them – as over a parapet – and on to the dark, Provençal landscape, beyond. There, the sliver of a moon hung – garlic-white – over the Luberon, while the very last stars still wobbled in their stations. Shimmered against the first, dark fires of dawn.

Of all the stars, Guido's favourites were those in Cassiopeia. He no longer associated that constellation, however, with the letter 'W', its distinguishing characteristic, but with that very same letter reversed. With that 'M' which might have stood for so many things, but in Guido's mind referred exclusively to the first initial of that still unattained, perhaps forever unattainable creature: the one whose heavy hair owned orchards and wellsprings, whose fingers spread across so many terraced vineyards and oak groves: la patrona *herself in all her attributes.*

'There,' he murmured to the distant stars in that marked, Piedmontese dialect of his. 'We're getting there bit by bit, aren't we?'

He'd begin by chipping the outer face of a rectangular block into a rough curve so that it matched – aligned – with the others. That it took on the roundness of the tower itself. Then, with a long, wood-handled rasp (a chemin de fer *set – at oblique angles – with so many razors), he pared down its unfinished surface. Brought it, thus, to a smoothness.*

'For you, Marguerite,' he murmured, as – by the small light of dawn – he eyed that ungainly block into position. Tested it for flushness. 'That's one more for you,' he said. Then added, as its absolute corollary, 'and one – one less – for me.'

He glanced upwards, at that very instant, as if he were

47

addressing more the 'M' that hung in those fading heavens than the plump absentee herself. Then, returning to his masonry, he poured a thin, liquid cement mixture into the branch-like channels he'd gouged into the facing – the recipient – stone, just beneath. Bright white, the channels flooded. Then, over this, he carefully slid his freshly prepared stone, sealing it, thereby – once and for all – into place.

With the second block, he repeated the procedure. If the first of the two, however, faced outwards, the second faced into the dovecote proper. These matched stones would have been carved as a single block if Guido had had an assistant, even a young apprentice, to help lift it into place. But he hadn't, and the weight of that single stone, for Guido, would have been well beyond his capacity.

Dawn was coming on quickly, now. And from his scaffold – his raised perch – Guido Stampelli could readily count the number of blocks still needed to complete a circle. To finish a ring, a rangée, of stones, whereby he'd gain access – at last – to that key, those steps, that doorway, that room. Gain access to what – even in his wildest fantasies – he couldn't imagine. Couldn't begin to imagine: that dark, forbidden experience whose very power might have resided, precisely, in the fact that it escaped the confines of the imagination itself, and lay at the furthest, outlying reaches of a still unassailable taboo.

Yes, only eight stones were needed, now, to close the circle. For Guido, this translated into four more days (or, rather, four more dawns) of masonry before Marguerite St Chamas's proposal would, at last, become valid, not to say – quite simply – granted. He lowered himself down off the scaffold, now, just as the clocktower of Lacoste struck seven in so many flat, irresonant strokes. 'Four more, Guido,' he murmured to himself as he scraped his trowel clean, and knocked off whatever cement still clung

48

to his galvanized pail. 'Four more to go,' he promised himself, as if at the end of that period he'd be entering not so much the locked bedroom of a particular woman, as the magic city itself. As some ultimate citadel. For, in Guido's dreams, it was just that. In them, the locked bedroom wasn't built out of solids: out of the stone and brick and timber he was so familiar with, but out of fluids alone. Out of the continuous flow and even distribution of so many luminous fluids. Yes – as Guido imagined it – it was alight. The bedroom was awash with its own, flowing light.

It was dawn, now. Guido Stampelli had already been up over four hours carving, gouging, transporting those twin limestone blocks, then levering them into place, before chipping, rasping, then finally cementing them into the pigeonnier's seemingly unaltered mass. His morning's work, now, for Marguerite St Chamas was finished. And his normal, six-day-a-week, twelve-hour-a-day workday could, at last, begin.

Yes, he thought, watching the horizon turn rose, then washed jonquil. His workday, at last, could begin.

6

'Wait, though,' she asked him.
    'Of course,' he said.
'Just a bit, a bit longer, Guy, won't you?'
'Whenever,' he assured her. 'It's thanks to you – after all – I'm writing it. That the whole thing's happening.'
    'Yes, yes, but save it,' she said. 'Save it, Guy,' she added, 'until the very end. Until it's all entirely finished, won't you?' With her head nestled in the crook of his shoulder, he could feel the bristle of her cropped, blonde hair against his tanned skin. It felt cool, astringent. He moved his shoulder, now, in such a way so as to feel it all the more keenly.
    'Until,' she continued, 'the whole, wonderful tower is finished. Then, then I'll want it. I'll want all of it, all at once,' she told him. He had an arm wrapped loosely about her naked waist. Now, pressing himself firmly against her, the two of them seemed to form a single, unbroken contour.
    'Frédérique,' he whispered into the tiny, gold whorl of her ear. And she – as if in response – drove her own hips even deeper into that unbroken contour. Fitted into it even tighter.

They'd been meeting clandestinely, now, for several weeks. They'd rendezvous each Thursday in one small hotel or roadside *auberge* after another, changing the place of their assignations continuously to avoid – or at least lessen – the risk of detection. Quite aside from the simple excitement they both felt in constantly exchanging rooms, hotels, entire towns, Frédérique insisted on preserving as much anonymity as possible. It was Frédérique, after all, who was still married. Who still had a 'reputation' to protect. By arriving as mere tourists or passing lovers, they wouldn't accumulate – she felt – those telltale traces, those tiny deposits of seeming trivia that – swept together, week after week, by some chambermaid or bartender – could turn into so much hardened, irrefutable fact.

Something more, however, was involved. For beyond the scrutiny of chambermaids and bartenders, Frédérique was intent on escaping that of her very own person. Her very own identity. Each Thursday, she wanted to come free of every constraint that held her not only to a husband and a fully grown daughter, but to anything that might still constitute what – somewhat disdainfully – she'd refer to as her 'past'. She went so far as to tell Fallows, on their very first rendezvous, that she even wanted to change names. To be called – whenever they met – by any name whatsoever, she said, except her own.

'Anything, anything you wish,' she said laughingly. 'You choose.'

'But you're not serious, are you?'

They were seated, that day, in the shaded terrace of a small, somewhat stately hotel (*un ancien hôtel particulier*), situated in the heart of Carpentras. Together, they were having drinks beneath a trellis, heavy – just then – with so many blossoming clusters of silver-blue wisteria. She looked up, suddenly, with that stunningly clear, incisive expression of hers, and said, 'I'm never not serious. That's something, I suppose, you'll have to learn.'

She was smiling as she said it, but Fallows could sense an

unmistakable undercurrent of determination in the tenor of her voice. For him, though, her true name (the name he'd known her by, no matter how offhandedly) had long since gelled about the shape of her face, the shadow of her extraordinarily long eyelashes, and yes, even the scent of honeysuckle she invariably smelt of. Her name, her very presence – for him – had become indissociable.

'You know, there's quite a choice,' he said lightheartedly. 'Where would you like me to begin?'

She looked down. And there, once again, were those lovely eyelashes, fanned against her cheeks like the elongated cilia of some elegant marine polyp. There, too, was that blonde hair he'd seen, only weeks earlier, shimmering in the open window-doors of her home in Ménerbes. That afternoon, it had flashed green. Had reflected off the long, chestnut leaves, just beyond, as she murmured – more to the leaves themselves than to Guy – about her father: about his memory, the ineffaceable memory of her unforgivable father.

Her eyes, now, as if swam up to meet his. She was smiling, once again, the lines at the edge of her eyes finely wrinkled. 'Maybe,' she said, hesitating a bit, 'maybe you might think up something a bit boyish,' she suggested. '*Quelque chose d'un peu garçon.*'

When, however, an instant later, he suggested 'Dominique', she dismissed the idea with a tiny shake – a quiver, really – of her blonde head. 'Lucienne' received the same dismissal, as did three or four other proposals. When, though, a moment later, Guy Fallows suggested 'Frédérique', she neither approved, at first, nor disapproved. Rather, she hesitated. She seemed to be tasting the word on her tongue, on her lips, against the cleft of her palate as if she were sampling a green wine, or some new, freshly arrived variety of oyster.

'Frédérique,' she whispered into the air about her, then

– in the same instant – as if caught within the privacy of her own hearing. She seemed to be testing the name for its least vibration. 'Say it yourself, Guy. Say "Frédérique".'

So he did, and she smiled deeply.

'Now,' she said, 'say it here,' pointing to the delicate whorl of her ear. 'Whisper it, Guy. Let me hear how it sounds.' So, holding her loosely about the shoulders, he as if fed those three, clipped syllables into that tiny vortex: *'Frédérique, Frédérique, est-ce que ça te plaît? Ça te plaît, ma belle Frédérique?'*

From that afternoon onwards, they'd never again refer to her previous – her authentic – name. Nor would either of them, from that day forth, mention her husband, or her daughter, or their house in Ménerbes, or any of the circumstances that had determined her life over the past few years. They'd entered – in a sense – into a fiction of their own. And, from that very afternoon, they'd begun thriving at its very heart. It was this, in fact, that Frédérique wanted to protect from all else. This that kept her, several weeks later, from listening to the very first chapters of Guy Fallows's novel. She didn't want *his* fiction (dealing as it did with her family) interfering, in any way, with *theirs*. For Frédérique's new name had given them (Guy, indirectly, as much as Frédérique) a licence of sorts, a permission to enter into a space in which each of them – freed of so much personal history – felt as if magically admitted. Their only reference – suddenly – had become themselves.

'Say it, say it,' she begged him teasingly. For it was like a new dress that she couldn't stop putting on, then taking off. She felt infused with this new-found persona. The name had endowed her with a freshness, a virginity of sorts that – a few days earlier – she could scarcely have imagined.

That afternoon, the two of them made love with a

continuously self-regenerating passion such as neither had ever known. Guy entering, Frédérique entered, they exulted in their discovery: of a life, suddenly unfettered. Released. A boundlessness arising out of so much freshly invented identity.

'Tell me that it won't stop. Won't simply dissolve,' she pleaded.

'It won't,' he promised, hearing his own voice catch in the steady, oar-like syncopation of their interlocked bodies.

'That we won't go backwards, either. Oh say it, Guy.'

'We won't, I promise you,' he said.

'That you won't send me back to my name, my forgotten name, oh promise me that you won't.'

'Never, I promise you, my beloved,' he said.

'That nothing will change.'

'Nothing,' he said.

'That we'll always be exactly like this, like an island unto ourselves. No clothes, no constraints, nothing but our naked selves. But the bed linens, just like little waves, lapping on all sides of us, oh promise.'

So he promised, knowing full well that Frédérique, bound by the rigours of her marriage to a daily routine, would be obliged to leave the hotel in no more than twenty minutes, now. She'd need to be impeccably groomed, as always, with every trace of their love-making washed free not only from her slender limbs, but from her breath, her voice, and – perhaps, most tellingly – from the weight and buoyancy of her blue gaze.

'Once more, just whisper it,' she begged.

So he did. He hissed it into the very labyrinth of her hearing, that it might lodge there like a dart, or the gold scroll – the engraved motto – of some pagan annunciation. 'Frédérique, Frédérique,' he hissed, almost silently.

And, as he did, she as if rose, exulting once again in the resonance of her new name.

She'd matured, like so many young women of her generation, in the shadow of her own doubts, hesitations. Unfailingly, she'd proceeded by an unbroken series of demi-measures, diluting whatever faith, questioning whatever assurance she might have had in her own abilities. And those abilities, in actual fact, were considerable. First in her class for three years running at the Faculté de Médecine at Montpellier, she wavered only when, at the end of those three years, she was confronted with the first of several critical decisions. Then, and each time thereafter, she chose what she desired least. Undermining herself in the face of so many single-minded young men, who seemed ready to sacrifice everything for the sake of a narrow – ever narrower – field of study, she moved from molecular biology (her original passion) to neurology. From neurology, after a somewhat indifferent year, she drifted (more out of laziness than out of any deliberate choice) into phytology. And there, for the moment, anyway, she seemed to settle. Studying the medicinal properties of plants in general, she began, after a first year, writing her doctoral dissertation on some obscure Amazonian subspecie, and its potential application in the treatment of potassium deficiency. She'd already written, in fact, well over 300 pages, and spent endless months in solitary laboratory research, when – quite unexpectedly – she abandoned the project altogether. She'd simply awoken, one morning, and decided that she'd be better suited, instead, teaching schoolchildren elementary botany in some local *lycée*.

It would be a decision she'd bitterly regret. For beyond every other consideration that touched upon a career in medicine (the income, the prestige, the degree of personal autonomy that that career would have provided), she'd never entirely forgive herself for abandoning – three-quarters completed – her doctoral dissertation. It went on to haunt her, in fact – year after year – like some unborn child. Like a foetus that she could neither abort, and be rid of, nor bring – ultimately – to term. It was, in a sense, her ghost. Her discomfort. And not even the birth of her own daughter, several years later, would relieve her of that muffled gnawing at her innards. That slight but incessant reminder.

Then, so many years later, she met Fallows. More, perhaps, than his charm and his tall, somewhat taciturn presence, she was drawn to him by the simple fact that he wrote books. Wrote, and – what's more – completed them. *Livre*, she thought. *Livre, délivre, délivre-moi de mon livre*, she mused, as he stood there, a good head taller, sipping quietly at his pastis. Furthermore, the very subject of his new novel touched directly upon her own past: the places of her childhood, the domain itself of her first reveries. Help him? Of course she'd help him, she immediately answered. And in whatever way that she could.

At first, she let him read letters, deeds, notarized documents that she'd managed to unearth: any mention whatsoever of that pink farmhouse and its outlying dovecote, freckled – each spring – in so much gold lichen. Then, one afternoon, over a table littered with papers, their bare arms happened to cross. Happened to cross, graze, then simply linger in the luxury of one another's contact. That very instant – in fact – their relationship turned, spontaneously, from one of archival curiosity to that – unabashed – of declared passion. And, only a week later, into a full-fledged love affair of its own.

With the advent of that affair, however, Frédérique's interest in Guy Fallows's novel – curiously enough – began to fade. Go under. For wasn't it, bit by bit, being replaced by their own? By their own, weekly fiction? Wasn't she

– after all – 'Frédérique' now, and didn't they, each Thursday, meet and make love and whisper heatedly about a world of their own invention? Yes, a book in fact of their own making? Didn't they? she kept asking.

Any mention of her past, or her parents' past – she well recognized – would undermine her new identity. That still fragile, still tenuous role she'd so recently assumed. Her two 'lives', she felt, had to be kept separate at all costs. Like two wires, they mustn't touch. Her past and present, as she called them, shouldn't at any point meet.

So, as their own fiction grew, Guy Fallows's novel fell gradually into eclipse. Fallows, of course, went on writing it. But every time he'd ask Frédérique to listen to a passage here, a chapter there, she'd hesitate. 'Save it,' she'd say. 'Save it, Guy, until it's finished.' No, she couldn't bear the idea of having him describe the very world she was so intent, now, on escaping. Not yet. Not yet, at least, she kept saying to herself. All she wanted, each Thursday, was to plunge – entire – into a *vita nuova* of their own. Yes, into a novel, a fiction of their own making.

Fallows, nonetheless, persevered. 'Stone by stone, syllable by syllable,' he watched – each week – his *pigeonnier* go up. He knew that Frédérique, some day, would want it, as well. Would stop fleeing into that fantasy they'd created for themselves, each Thursday, and want – even need – the sharp, delineated world he was reconstituting, day after day, with such painstaking care. That world, that space – after all – was hers. Hers from birth.

Furthermore, Fallows realized that if Guido had been the source of this entire work, Frédérique was its inspiration. Towards her, each week, the tower rose. Into that aroma of honeysuckle, the stones of his prose – block after block – clambered, jostled for space, worked their way, finally, into a single, ascendant form. That very week, in fact,

57

in describing Guido, Fallows realized that the force that drove his words forward wasn't – entirely – his. He'd been, for some time now, literally inspired. His words, along with Guido's steps, seemed to rise of their own volition. For Guido, at long last, had pulled the key with its green ribbon out from under the stone trough, and – for the very first time – taken the exterior staircase up to Marguerite St Chamas's bedroom. More, perhaps, than inspired, Guy felt guided. For wasn't it Frédérique – Frédérique's presence in his every breath – that brought Guido, now, on to the landing? That brought him to raise his hand, just then, to that low, nail-larded door that stood, locked, before him? Locked, but inwardly – as agreed – unbolted. Yes, it drew Guido's hand, now (the hand itself not large but permanently swollen, having dealt – all its life – with so much abrasive mass) flush with the door. Yes, it brought Guido, that very instant, to knock.

He knocked, then waited, Guy Fallows read. *Then knocked, once again. Guido knew, of course, that even if he knocked all night (it was only twilight at the time, and from the landing where he stood, he could still differentiate – far beyond – the small almond orchards from the even smaller olive groves, standing stout, iridescent, domed), no one could possibly hear him. He went on, however, knocking gently, regularly, without any insistence whatsoever, half hoping that the* patrona *(who, of course, in any case, couldn't hear) wouldn't hear. Wouldn't notice. He who'd dreamt, fixated, upon that one moment to the exclusion of all else, who'd laboured for that very instant over the past three weeks, laboured by nobody's light but the moon's and his own few candles, found himself dully knocking, now, upon that door as one might knock – dolefully – on the planks of a coffin.*

And dead, seemingly, she was. For once within – once, that is, Guido Stampelli had yielded to the realization that

*there was no way of avoiding the very object of his own
inflamed passion, of annulling so much scarcely contained,
containable lust, but to use the key that had been provided
for exactly those satisfactions – he'd found, lit by the low,
pendulous globe of a spirit lamp, Marguerite St Chamas's
inert body. It lay on its bed, back turned, underneath the
long, grey wave of a coverlet. Startled, Guido made as if to
move. But there was nowhere – he well knew – to escape
to. Everything was* there. *Was* present. *That sack, that
bundle of seemingly intransigent matter, that agglomerate
of hair and organ and muscle fibre, its shoulders wrapped
in a blouse, or bathrobe, or – for all Guido knew –
some shroud, was, in fact, his lodestone. His north. And
everything within him, now, was directed – magnetically
– towards it. He couldn't retract.*

*Nor did he. He removed his shoes (but only his shoes),
and left them – perfectly paired – at the base of a tall, straw-
backed armchair. Then, having stepped silently across the
tiled floor, he crawled up on to the high, four-poster bed.
The bed – the whole room, he suddenly realized – smelt
acrid with camphor. Guido himself felt as if caught in that
odour. In its thin, caustic signal. He'd entered it as one
might enter some poisonous gas: he hadn't the choice.*

*Crawling on his back now, across the grey folds of the
coverlet, he moved like a sandcrab: on the points of his
elbows, that is, and the balls of his feet. The closer he came,
however, the smaller his 'steps' grew. For, approaching that
heap, that indeterminate mass of a biologically indeterminate nature, he found himself confronted by an obstacle
(and, in turn, a fresh set of inhibitions) he might well
have foreseen. For how, he asked himself, could he lay
a hand – no matter how lightly – upon whatever it was
that seemed to sleep there (was it really* her? *was it really
hers, that swollen outline?) and not – in some material
sense – violate that house, those fields, the undulant fold*

of so much endless vineyard? How could he touch the one, he wondered, without ravishing the other? For – in Guido Stampelli's mind – the two were inseparable. Once, he remembered, while 'talking' with Marguerite St Chamas, he'd noticed how the very tips of her plump fingers had come to rest on an armchair. The chair, the waxed tiles it stood on, the very light – that instant – that flooded the room, had become – in Guido's mind – not only hers, but her. *She not only owned them, he felt, she infused them, saturated each with her own, overwhelming presence. And that presence, in Guido's mind, had become – to its last, quivering branch, its final, flowering canebreak – inviolable.*

He'd reached her, now. In fact, he was lying, propped on his elbows, directly alongside her. He was close enough to her tightly bound head of red hair – to those braided ropes of deep Titian – to smell the eau de toilette *it had been sprinkled in. It smelt – pungently – of roses. And, as the scent of those roses as if burnt its way through that of the ambient camphor, Guido Stampelli brought his face up against its soft, redolent source. Doing so, he felt, or rather sensed – coming from that bundled mass – the slightest tremor, a twinge really, like that – in mid-summer – of distant lightning. Yes, a quiver, and nothing more. But for Guido, it was enough. It indicated life. It indicated – no matter how mutely – some form, some covert sign, of response.*

Yes, no matter how slight, the twinge as if tore through that chrysalid of inhibitions, that tissue of constraints, and laid bare, in Guido, the latent organism of total intent. He pressed his body hard, now, against that heavily clad mass, and in no more than five, six, rhythmic heaves of his buttocks forward, felt the successive leap of his own, irrepressible releases. Felt them as they flashed and puddled, warm now across the flat of his belly. Then,

60

*unabated, without an instant's interruption, Guido went
under. Pulling his trousers off first, and the wet, already
chilling film of his underpants, he slid – half-naked –
between the coarse linens. And, as he did, he came up flush
against her. Against all that bundled inertia. Immediately,
he began drawing, tugging (with an impossible composite
of deference and aggression) at the heavy skirt she'd
insisted on wearing, even beneath the cover of her own
bedclothes. Awkwardly, he rolled the skirt upwards. He
gathered it – best as he could – like a fat hoop, or a wrapped
turban, about the level of her waist. Just underneath, she
was as naked as he.*

*That night, he never stopped. He made love to Mar-
guerite St Chamas over and over, entering her sex from
the only angle that presented itself: from, that is, behind.
(Like a great house, he might have thought. Like some*
grande bastide *that a labourer, such as himself, might
enter only from behind, yes, he probably thought, like
that. Exactly like that.) While she, in turn – as Guido
drove and retracted, pulsated regularly within her – simply
lay there. Never moved. With the spirit lamp having long
since guttered, gone out, she lay – face to the wall – in
the darkness of her own bedroom, seemingly impassive,
imperturbable. She never gave the smallest sign of pleasure,
nor – for that matter – displeasure. Not a throb, a spasm,
nothing now that might indicate that she wasn't asleep,
or – far more – hadn't fallen into some profound and,
ultimately, irreversible coma.*

'*Guido, that night, never saw her,*' Guy Fallows read – out
loud – from his novel. Read – out loud, now – to no one, if
not the empty armchair, facing him. '*He smelt her, though.
He smelt the rose* eau de toilette *that she'd sprinkled her
hair with, the scent of which fuelled his own, high passion
even higher. But he never, in fact, saw – in the dark of that*

61

room, her face facing the dark of that wall – how, over and over, her mouth had twisted. How – convulsive – it had rounded into an immense, endlessly mute scream of sheer release. Nor would he feel, rushing through her, its repercussions,' Guy Fallows read. *'No, never once would he even begin to imagine how her lips – in those moments – had spread. Had rolled into a swollen orifice not unlike the worn marble spout on the village fountainhead, its flanks lashed by the sinuous tails of two, frolicking dolphins.*

'No, he'd never know this,' Guy Fallows read – out loud – to the empty armchair, facing him. *'Never know that the screams – wild, unretainable, unendingly mute – had ever existed.'*

7

Twice, he thought. I've tried it twice, he said to himself, sitting at the edge of his fireplace, poking embers loose from the underside of a burning log. He watched how the embers fell, hissing as they did in a soft, incandescent shower, on to the black hearth below. Yes, twice, and never mentioned it, either. Never told her, he added, as he beat the still flickering embers into an even bed of low, glowing coals. Perhaps now, he wouldn't need to, what's more. What with the *pigeonnier* beginning to rise – chapter by chapter – and, along with it, his spirits, his confidence, and yes, yes, most of all, his love, perhaps now – indeed – he wouldn't need to.

Mention what? Perhaps the one thing on earth that Guy Fallows couldn't name himself. That numbness, that nihility, that corrosive indifference in his heart of hearts that had brought him, one night, to take a whole bottle of barbiturates without a single forethought. That had broken down every distinction between life and death so that it no longer seemed to matter whether he found himself on this side, or that. Either way, a landscape without colour, contour, without any relief whatsoever, seemed to spread endlessly before him.

The second time – at least – there'd been forethought. Even rage. After six months of utter impasse on a new novel, not to mention an overriding sense that his entire lifetime had been nothing but waste, Fallows – quite deliberately – drove his car off a cliff. His son, only seven at the time, was spending the summer, then, with his grandparents. And Guy, quite alone, and still suffering from the loss of a woman he felt to be utterly irreplaceable, had been drinking himself into a total stupor. One day, he realized that he'd had enough. Enough – that is – of himself. His thoughts, at that hour, were still clear, and his resolve entire. He got into his car, and sped off. It didn't take long. Accelerating through a tight curve in the mountains, his car flew off the edge of the road, and bounced – five, six, seven times – down the lopsided boulders of a deep ravine. When the car caught fire at the base of the ravine, Fallows wasn't in it. He'd been thrown clear after the first impact, and had landed in a thicket of boxwood with several broken ribs and a collapsed kidney.

Twice, he thought. Twice, I've gone under. But now, as he sat there, years later, raking the embers evenly over the floor of the hearth, he could feel that fragile, newfound confidence rising, gradually, within him. For weeks, now, he'd felt it. Felt it rising from so many pages of accomplished work. Like a bouquet, patiently gathered out of its disparate parts, he'd begun assembling his *pigeonnier*, putting into words what Guido Stampelli, half a century earlier, had carved into so much weight-less stone.

'For you,' he whispered, out loud. For the one who wasn't there. The one whose blonde hair went green in the reflected light of so many sun-splashed leaves. Whose thighs – even – smelt of honeysuckle.

'For you,' he repeated, happy – even in her absence – to be addressing her.

Now with the embers spread to a smooth bed of glow-ing coals, he set four lamb chops to grill over the low, matted fire. Through its wire grates, the lamb spat and crackled. And the bristling rosemary it was seasoned in – its stiff bevy of quills – began to curl into so many black, calcinated hooks. As it did, the whole room filled with the aroma.

Guy Fallows, now, took a long sip of wine. Throughout the day, there was a glass – invariably – at his elbow, and whether he was writing or reading, or – as at present – simply cooking, a plain goblet of what he called his *gros rouge* seemed to follow him about like an itinerant fixture. He drank less, now. Much less. But he still needed a continuous trickle of those dark, distilled juices. Still counted on the wine's effect for maintaining a certain level of consciousness. Still – in short – needed it.

He was, in fact, just opening a second litre of that *gros rouge*, when the telephone rang. He knew exactly who'd be calling.

'I don't think I'll be able to make it for dinner,' the voice said, gently. 'But I'll be there, later on. Some time later, I imagine,' it said.

Guy Fallows, who insisted – in both his life and work – on a high level of explicitness, found his son's round, amorphous phrases, as always, irritating. It wasn't, however, only his son – his son's way of expressing himself – that vexed him. An entire generation of young people had, it seemed, drifted free of the basic tenets of language, and begun expressing themselves – more and more – in what Fallows called the rhetoric of the muffled, the opaque. Sometimes it seemed that only the vaguest outlines of coherent statement still managed to survive, and even those – at times – appeared menaced. It wasn't, Fallows realized, so much laziness, or semi-illiteracy, as a common distrust – amongst the young – of the world, the articulated world that they were about to inherit. They were refusing, it seemed to Fallows, the very *terms* of that inheritance.

'Will I see you later this evening?' the father asked.

'It depends,' the son answered in that same, gentle voice of his. 'It all depends,' he repeated, then ended the conversation with a long string of inconclusives.

Andrew Fallows was living, 'more or less', with Vic Daubigny, Solange Daubigny's daughter. A good deal taller than her mother, Vic not only dressed in black – that banner of a whole generation's distress – but had dyed her hair (which was naturally as blonde as her mother's) a black verging on a deep, metallic blue. Together, the two of them, Vic and Andrew, lived in a kind of informal inseparability. They came and went, talked vaguely of voyages, of whole continents they'd some day travel to that – for them – didn't seem to have any geographic bearings whatsoever. The continents were as afloat as they themselves. Together, though, with one another, they remained unfailingly kind, attentive. Despite that vaporous world that seemed to surround them, inwardly they formed a tiny, complicitous tribe unto themselves. *Une tribu à deux.*

So, as he often did, Guy Fallows ate by himself. To keep his lamb chops warm, he left them alongside the fire in which they'd just grilled. Then, he began his meal – as the peasantry still does in Provence – with fresh salad. He turned the leaves of the salad over inside a deep, olive-wood bowl, the inner flanks of the bowl scrubbed in garlic and saturated – from so many years of use – with so much gold, cold-pressed oil. He scarcely needed to add to those past deposits, either: the leaves, already, exuded the bouquet. Then, with a fork in one hand, and a scrap of *pain de campagne* in another, he entered into that nightly ritual, washing down leaf, bread, and a *ratatouille* he'd let simmer over the low, blinking coals, with so many swallows of that dark, and – for Fallows – indispensable *rouge*.

Each night, in fact, he'd let himself go. He'd let the wine steadily – infallibly – deliver him from the still persistent residue of his own doubts. From so many years spent questioning his own worth. Yes, Fallows still 'needed it'. Would still feel, with each, successive glass, a certain recurrent tension dissipate. Feel his nerves as if unknot.

He was free to think, now, of his novel. To think of Frédérique, as well, in so many loose, ongoing frames of released imagery. No, he said to himself: think of Frédérique later. Once the shutters are latched and the lights out. Once there's nothing but wind in the red waves of the roof-tiles, overhead, and your body – the full length of your body – lying against that lovely, imaginary imprint. Wait. Wait until then.

And that's exactly what he did. He ate his lamb chops and finished his dinner on dry, salty wedges of goat's cheese. The wedges flaked off his Opinel like so much desiccated soap. Washing them down now, he thought about the upcoming chapter of his novel. For the next chapter, he knew, would be heavily charged. He'd have to disclose – at the very outset – how Emmanuel St Chamas, in fleeing for his life, had left his spouse not only penniless, but pregnant. Yes, after five years of marriage, Emmanuel St Chamas would have finally succeeded. He'd at last have impregnated his wife, and – in so doing – cleared himself of what he considered the most pernicious of all rumours (far worse, he felt, than those touching on his fascist affiliations): the one, that is, that questioned his own virility.

By the time, however, that Marguerite St Chamas's pregnancy had become common knowledge throughout the countryside, St Chamas himself would have already vanished. Would have already found refuge in some jungle mission in the very heart of the Cameroons.

From that point, Guy Fallows reflected – finishing, as he did, his cheese with a deep draft of wine – his chapter would turn to Guido. To Marguerite and Guido. To how, through the fall of 1944 and the winter of 1945, Guido would follow, with the flat of his hand, the gradual swelling of Marguerite St Chamas's belly. How it would 'ripen', as he might have said, through the passing months, as – month after month – Guido (his visits, each twenty-four days, falling with all the faultless regularity of tides, of lunar phases) would make his way up those very same steps. The green ribbon – once again – as if dripping from his wrist, he'd knock upon that door that was no more, no less, sentient to sound than *la patrona* herself. He'd knock, as much out of fear as simple respect, on that low, nail-larded door, then wait. Wait a long, self-imposed moment before, finally, entering. Within, he'd leave his shoes, once again, paired alongside that same stiff-backed armchair, then join Marguerite St Chamas or, rather, the heap in which she was so totally assimilated, high upon her wide, four-poster bed.

Fallows had decided, sitting there, jotting down notes on odd pieces of paper, that he'd portray Guido as someone secretly proud of Marguerite St Chamas's pregnancy. Even if he hadn't been its cause, he'd feel – by proximity alone – deeply implicated. For Guido would have had a peasant's reverence for whatever was fertile, be it a root, or a pod, or a full-grown, full-bearing female. Then, too, as an Italian, he'd have been inculcated, since birth, on images of the Virgin: icons in which the palm of her hand would be resting – but scarcely – against that domed tumescence. That bulge that rose – celestial blue – from underneath the folds of her gown. Guido, in turn, would come to consider every pregnant woman as a reincarnation, in sort, of that Mother of Miracles.

Yes, Guy Fallows thought, that's how he'd proceed. He

68

went on writing notes – that evening – to his forthcoming chapter: bits of dialogue, scenery, graphic detail. On the back of envelopes, inside the empty cardboard boxes of his cigarillos, Guy Fallows sketched out one passage after another:

How Guido, no matter how hard he'd scrub himself, no matter what soaps he'd use, would always smell of rabbit and woodsmoke. Would smell – ineffaceably – of that elemental kitchen he cooked in, night after night. Of its meats, its fires.

How each successive visit to Marguerite St Chamas's bedroom would both repeat the previous visit, and – at the same time – introduce some slight variant. Some risk, for instance, that Guido might take. Some yet untested gesture.

How one night, for example, he might finally work up enough courage to undo Marguerite St Chamas's piled hair. How, passively, she'd comply.

How, as the hair came tumbling undone, Guido would plunge his face into its unloosened mass, and murmur – as he did – into that sprinkled odour of roses. That rich thicket.

Never once, however, would she turn. Never once would she acknowledge Guido's presence. How, lying there, her face to the wall, as apparently indifferent as she was – indeed – mute, she'd receive Guido exactly as a drain might receive so much unabated flash flood.

Not even now would Guido see how her mouth contorted. Rounded into something wild, uncontained: into the 'O' of so many deep, repeated satiations.

No, he'd never know. Never guess how much she lusted after those visits – each twenty-four days – at least as much as he did himself. Perhaps more.

As the months passed, however, the nature of Guido's passion would gradually change. Grow increasingly tender, protective, as Marguerite St Chamas – month after month – swelled towards delivery.

69

Would grow increasingly paternal, as well. For, feeling the foetus's tiny, haphazard kicks as it entered its fifth month, Guido would come to love this 'little, blindfolded stranger', as he called it, as if it were his own.

Never, though, would Marguerite St Chamas give Guido the least sign. Never the smallest acknowledgment.

How, during this period, Guido's work on the pigeonnier *would go on uninterruptedly. And, by the spring of 1945, the tower would have risen to well over a third its completed height. Would have taken on, in so doing, a certain 'allure'.*

How, unexpectedly, in the eighth month of her pregnancy, Marguerite St Chamas would vanish. The foreman at the huge, sprawling, and now essentially inactive farmhouse, would have been advised that she'd left for Nice; that she'd remain there, as well, until some time after childbirth.

Guido, of course, would go on building. Would complete one rangée *of stone and begin on another. Would complete the second, and still – dawn after dawn, without any 'recompense' now whatsoever, without even the least word from her who once proffered 'recompense' – wouldn't falter. Would go on building.*

He might even come to consider his work on the tower as a contribution, a 'gift' of sorts, both to the mother and – soon enough – to the child, as well. Both to Marguerite St Chamas and that little foetus of hers that he'd come so terribly close, indeed, to fathering himself.

Here, Guy Fallows stopped. He spread his notes out, like so many playing cards, across the oil-cloth cover of his dining-room table. Then – one at a time – he read them through. Each of them touched upon some essential moment in his forthcoming chapter. He sat there drinking, thinking of that chapter, and – by extension – of the whole novel itself. He thought, too, of Frédérique, for whom he was writing the novel: building his own *pigeonnier* very much as Guido, once, had built his for Marguerite St Chamas. Some day, too, she'd want it, Guy realized. Some day, the novel would give to the ambivalence of that life – the drift of her days – the kind of grounding Frédérique so desperately needed. Yes, some day, he realized, his novel would put an end to her fiction.

'Frédérique,' Guy mumbled to himself. He was thinking, at that very moment, of her long lashes. Their incredible curl.

'Frédérique, Frédérique,' he went on, whispering to nothing, really, but the tremor that ran – parched – through his lips.

The glass at his elbow, now, was no longer filled with wine, but *marc*: that pale honey-coloured alcohol drawn from the waste of so much already pulverized pip and grapeskin. It was this: this thin, lethal fluid that Guy Fallows employed, each night, for the sole purpose of dissolving those doubts, those tensions that still – residually – troubled his being. It was this, this *marc*, that allowed him – after a certain hour, each evening – to float as if free of himself. To come, in sorts, undone.

He might still have been mumbling 'Frédérique', a moment later, when he lay his head down on his arms and fell soundly asleep on his dining-room table. He wouldn't stir, either, until, dawn. Lying there in a pond of light that fell – bronze – from an overhead fixture, Fallows would never hear, for instance, how the wind, outside, had risen. How it blew, now, over the terracotta roof-tiles, and brought the shaggy tamarisk to brush – with its thick filaments – against his walls. Nor would he, in any way, be aware of how that same wind had washed the night sky to something so utterly immaculate. How each star in that sky, now, shone with such merciless precision. Such surgical exactitude. Never, in fact, as on nights like that (for those, that is, who'd remained awake) would the notion of divine intercession appear so inconceivable. What with the sky so high, so remote, burning in all its

71

fiery isolation, even the myth of those plumed intercessors (those that commuted, once, so readily between heaven and earth) would appear, now, as nothing more than naïve sublimation.

Yes, on nights like that, the heavens belonged exclusively to the heavens. And the earth, to the sleeping hordes of its unconsoled.

8

'And Gabrielle?' she asked, teasingly. 'What about Gabrielle?'

Fallows shook his head. His head lay nestled against the shaft of her neck, while his breath – steadily – blew out lightly over her slender collarbones. 'Wouldn't you love it, though?' she asked him. 'To hold me – just like this – and call me Gabrielle all through the night, oh wouldn't you?'

Fallows lay there, listening to her heartbeat. Listening, too, to how her breath rose and fell as if in the hollow trough of his own. How it cupped, and then – just as gently – crested. How – together – they as if pleasured in the same, invisible waters. In the haulage of an identical rhythm. He held her, now, even tighter.

'And Michelle,' she continued, 'there's Michelle, too,' she proposed, taunting Fallows with one ambivalent name after another. Only the slightest inflection kept each from being read as its opposite.

'And Pascale,' she asked, running its sound against the edge of his ear. 'How would you like to wake up, one morning, and find yourself lying alongside someone called Pascale? Someone "strange and exciting", as they say in novels? Well,' she asked with mock impatience, 'wouldn't you?'

Fallows knew that Frédérique was never more serious than when she appeared to be teasing, cajoling him. In moments like that, she was simply testing the ground about her. And that ground – Fallows well knew – was a continuously shifting quantity. It varied with the moment, the weather, with Frédérique's least susceptibility.

'Well,' she insisted, 'wouldn't you? We could close the shutters, and pretend that it's night, and later we could open them, and pretend that it's morning, and you could call me Michelle or Pascale or whatever name that you wished. Wouldn't that be marvellous, Guy? You could lie all morning inside me, and call me one name after another. And yes, there's Claude, there's Claude as well. You could call me "Claude, *mon adorée*", and fill me, fill me with yourself as you did. Oh, wouldn't you like that? To play with my earlobes, and whisper "Claude" into my ear, all morning, and fill me with yourself, oh Guy, wouldn't you?'

He didn't answer. He held her even closer, now, knowing that that closeness was a response in itself. Perhaps, too, he added, the only one befitting. Frédérique needed to be stilled. Needed to be held against that drift, that tug, that undertow that drew her – at times like this – with all the obscure dynamic of her own worst anxieties.

'There are so many names, so many wonderful names,' she said lazily, lying there against him, locked in the slow, cradled rhythm that they'd both adopted. 'Yes, so many names,' she whispered. 'One could go on and on . . .'

'But don't. Don't, Frédérique,' he said, breaking suddenly into his own silence. 'Don't,' he whispered with an urgency she could scarcely mistake.

'Don't let me, then,' she responded. 'Stop me. Stop me, Guy.'

She broke rhythm that very instant to look at Guy Fallows all the more intently. Propped up, now, on one elbow, she gazed down into his eyes. She seemed to be searching into their very depths as if to find – within them – some lost sign of herself. The fleeting trace of some buried reflection.

Without knowing exactly why, Fallows had always found that gaze – with its passionate focus – strangely disturbing. Nothing, it would seem, lay behind it. The gaze appeared to have no memory, no history, no precedents. Only that sharp, magnified lustre: the blue needlepoints of its own, probing insistence. That demanded – that very instant – an instantaneous response.

'Frédérique,' he whispered. 'My beautiful, blue-eyed Frédérique.'

'Yes, say it,' she pleaded. 'Say it over and over.'

And so he did. And the two of them, once again, entered into that intimate fiction they'd invented for themselves. 'Thursday's regimen', as they'd come to call it. And, as always, Frédérique thrived – thrived in the role of Frédérique that she'd been cast in. That afternoon, too, she played it with particular intensity. The name, no matter how fictive, had given her an identity – a sense of her own presence – such as she'd never known. It instilled in her, as well, an ardour, a kind of erotic lash, such as she never thought she possessed.

So the two of them, once again, became one, driving every cell of their being – that afternoon – into a single, impacted mass. A deep, rhythmic collusion.

Later, they lay apart, staring up at the fanciful, rose mouldings of their hotel bedroom. Outside, the sounds of Avignon barely reached them, muffled by the overlapping leaves of a massive plane tree, just beyond, and the drawn,

75

embroidered expanse of a pair of curtains, within. They lay, now, as if in the wash of their own, reciprocal releases. They could feel, as they did, that sudden calm overtake every part of their being. They seemed as if afloat, returning as they were into their separate selves. Even their voices sounded limp, removed, as they whispered to one another, now, in order not to disturb the depth of the other's stillness.

'Tell me,' she murmured, 'tell me that there's no one, that there's only me, only us. Tell me, Guy. I need to hear it.'

'There's no one,' he replied. 'I can assure you, there's absolutely no one.'

'Not even,' she suggested, 'Solange Daubigny?' She'd ask that very same question, now, every time they'd meet. Fallows, for his part, had come to expect it. It was like a particular passage in some recurrent rite.

'Not even,' he replied.

'Not even a little bit?' she tested. 'She's very attractive, after all, don't you find?'

'Very.'

'And every bit as charming. As charming as I am, wouldn't you say?'

'Every bit,' he agreed. 'But it's not Solange Daubigny I'm attracted to. Not even slightly.'

'Have you seen her eyes, though? How beautiful they are?'

'They're very beautiful.'

'And her ankles, her slender ankles? Have you?'

'I have,' he said, 'and her shanks, as well. The long, neat muscles of her shanks.'

'Then you *have* noticed, haven't you?'

'I notice everything,' Guy Fallows responded flatly. 'But it's not her I love. It's you.'

'I hate it, though, that you notice her ankles, and her

shanks, and what you call her long, neat muscles. It's *me* I want you to notice. *Me* I want you to love.'

She'd sat up and begun staring, once again, into Guy Fallows's eyes. Even at that close distance, however, she appeared – with her swept-back hair and her finely chiselled features – to be as if racing through wind, or water, or so much opaque shadow, in some desperate – even mythical – attempt to reach him. She whispered, now, into his mouth.

'Hate her. Hate her for my sake. It's *me* you should be noticing, not her. Notice my hands, now, what my hands are doing, can you feel that, and my lips? Notice my lips,' she insisted, as she bent over Guy Fallows, and Fallows rose into her words, and then into her silence, and called her – locked now in the depth of that silence – by the one name she wished to be called by.

'Frédérique, Frédérique,' he whispered heatedly. But she was far too taken, now, to respond.

Throughout the late spring and early summer, their love continued to bud, blossom, to take on – already – a precocious ripeness of its own. Much of that ripeness, Fallows well knew, was due to the little theatre – the *commedia* – that they'd created for themselves: those performances that, each week, grew more and more consummate. Frédérique, increasingly, flourished in the role of Frédérique. And Guy (ever more mindful, attentive, adoring) as – in sorts – her accomplice. For he could interpret, now, Frédérique's least humour. Could measure, and faultlessly, the finest thread of her most secret longing.

Each week, then, they came closer and closer to perfecting those roles. Establishing, as they did, out of an unwritten script, a reality of their own.

That reality, though, wasn't without its risks. Built as it was on a fabulation – on the use of a pseudonym and on so many scrupulously observed omissions – it left Frédérique increasingly dependent on Guy. For only Guy, in fact, could vouch for its existence. Could authenticate that role which – each week – Frédérique gave herself to with ever increasing abandon. And, as she did, as she invested that personage, now, with her very being, so too did her sense of her own identity grow increasingly fragile, tenuous. Of this, Guy was all too aware.

'I couldn't manage, now, without you,' she told him, one day. 'I simply couldn't.' They were standing, just then, in front of a small antique shop in the market town of L'Isle-sur-la-Sorgue. While Guy peered through the window at the bric-à-brac within, Frédérique seemed to be inspecting – in that very same window – their reflections. One was tall, sombre; the other – for her age – svelte, but aflame.

'Couldn't, simply couldn't,' she went on. She seemed to be addressing – in that soft, anxious voice of hers – no one, really, but herself.

'Look,' he said, 'just inside. Do you see that brooch, that garnet brooch? There, just to the left, in the blue velvet box? Isn't it lovely?' he asked, pointing it out.

'Couldn't manage, just couldn't,' she continued, as if deaf to everything but the echo of her own thoughts. 'There's no one but you, now, who knows me. Who'd recognize me. But you, Guy,' she said.

'Isn't it lovely, though,' he insisted, attempting – in some small way – to distract her from the solitary drift of her thoughts. From that isolation that – quite suddenly – seemed to divide them. 'Isn't it, though?' he persisted.

'No one, no one . . .' she went on, oblivious.

'Wouldn't you like it, Frédérique? Couldn't I get it for you?' he asked, pointing – once again – through the bright reflections, to that thin, geometric spray of garnets, within.

'Without you, you see, I'd float off the very edge . . .'

78

she said, deaf to everything – it seemed – but her own murmurs.

'It would look so stunning, pinned to your blouse.'

'. . . off the edge, the very edge . . .'

'The lapel, for instance, of your black satin blouse,' Fallows went on, assuredly, 'so perfectly stunning.'

'. . . and no one, not even you, finally, would recognize me. Look,' she murmured, as if addressing her own reflection, now. 'Look at those cheeks, those temples, that shingled hair. Frédérique, *your* Frédérique, could vanish just like that. With a gust of wind, be gone. There's nothing – nothing – to keep her.'

'Please,' Guy pleaded, '*fais-moi plaisir*. Let me get it for you.' He brought his arm about her shoulders, and she – as if in response – pressed her face against the rumpled blue of his linen jacket.

'Yes,' she replied, breaking – suddenly – her own spell. 'Go ahead. Get it for me, Guy. Get me anything, anything you wish,' she said exhaustedly. 'Yes, Guy, get it. Get it for me.'

And so he did. But something that day – that late Thursday in L'Isle-sur-la-Sorgue – had happened. And although Guy Fallows couldn't say exactly what, it marked – no matter how imperceptibly – the end of that budding, that blossoming, that coming of ripeness. For they'd already ripened, in fact, and now, utterly unaware, had entered into that slow but ineluctable decline. A turbidness, now, had invaded their love, it would seem. Had begun undermining that clarity, that limpidity, such as they'd known.

Yes, a cloud, rather than a worm, had made its way to the heart of the fruit. And the fruit – beginning that very week – would begin to darken, contract.

They met, as usual, the following Thursday, but – that afternoon – didn't make love. Frédérique blamed the wind

– an exceptionally high, mid-summer mistral – for what she called her 'indisposition'. She seemed particularly tense, restless, that day. Dressed in white – a white blouse and a pair of white, loose-hanging slacks – she'd draped about her shoulders an emerald green, Hermès shawl that gave a slightly icy, somewhat forbidding air to her overall appearance. Sitting in the far corner of a deep, deeply tufted sofa, her narrow frame as if moulded to its contours, she ran her fingertips up and down the piping of her shawl, or – occasionally – toyed with her gold wedding band. She'd twist, rub, grind the band about the slender shaft of her finger, describing – as she did – so many suffocating little circles.

'Forgive me,' she said, 'it must be the wind.'

'Of course,' he answered gently, standing by the tall window-doors.

'It can be so exhausting, even now. Even in the midst of summer, don't you find?'

'Of course,' he said. 'Of course I do.'

'It seems to work on one's nerves, wearing one down. It doesn't stop, either.'

'Why don't you get into bed, my love? Why don't you get into bed and have a good nap for yourself?'

'Would you mind, Guy? Would you?'

So she stripped down to her underclothes, then slid between the crisp blue sheets of the bed. Fallows could see her, now, in the mirrored cabinets, as she removed her underclothes as well, and flung them on to a facing armchair. Could see – several moments later – the very first ripples (twinges, really) as they travelled across the surface of that blue sheet. Could watch – in the angled mirror – as they gathered, rhythmic. Grew incessant, nearly monotonous now, out of the bed's very centre. The whole intimate spectacle, in fact, reminded Guy Fallows of someone plucking – obsessively – at a single note on some hidden, string instrument.

80

He'd seen it before. He knew, too, exactly what it meant. That search, he thought. They're always searching, aren't they – he asked himself – for something under. Beneath – even – their own pleasure. Even – perhaps – their own comprehension. And, in love, is it really us, he wondered, whom they love? Or the extent to which – sometimes – we awaken that darkness. Stir the shadows – occasionally – of that underworld. That double that seems to sleep in each of them. For Fallows himself had never known a woman, he now realized, who wasn't – in some way – pregnant with herself. With her own, inaccessible 'other'. Wasn't it *her*, that very moment, Frédérique was attempting to reach? Arouse? To please in whatever way she might? Stirring her own she-phoenix out of so much self-generated heat?

She'd put herself to sleep, now. Asleep, her head in the golden swath of her hair, she looked somewhat smaller, Guy Fallows remarked. She lay on one side with the blue sheet running taut – almost level – from her shoulder to her hip, then falling, in a single gradient, to the sharp point of her toes.

Fallows himself sat in an armchair, now, alongside. He'd been watching, for some time, the infinitesimal heave of her body as it rose and fell to her own breathing. Now, though, that she was asleep, he looked down at the open pages of his manuscript. They lay spread across his lap. He'd wanted to read them to Frédérique, for they touched, in fact, on the period of her birth, and the very first months of her life. Once again, though, that afternoon, she'd begged him to wait. Once again, on entering the bedroom, she'd found the perfect pretext, or excuse, for avoiding that 'encounter'. That 'reminder' of whom she'd been, as opposed to that creature – that second self – she so desperately wished to become. That *Frédérique* to the very last, awakened cell of her existence. 'No, not yet, Guy. Not quite yet,' she'd begged him.

So, as she slept, he leafed through the pages himself. Reviewing them, in a sense, as he went. They began with the description of her birth, forty-four years earlier, and – soon after – her arrival at that sprawling, rose stucco farmhouse. He went on to read of all the tiny but imperative accommodations that had to be made – for the infant's sake – in the midst of so much rural simplicity. Water, for instance, still had to be heated over a stove, and the stove itself continuously fed on so many small chunks of firewood. Diapers (torn tablecloths, in effect) needed to be boiled in a tall cauldron that a peasant girl oversaw as a chef might some simmering *marmite*. Into the cauldron, occasionally, she'd pour ash, the ash serving – as it had for centuries – as a natural, and highly effective, detergent.

Frédérique continued to sleep, now, as Fallows read. Read, in effect, of her very first months. How her mother, almost immediately, had hired a wet-nurse, refusing to exhaust her own energies (considerable as they were) on the infant's already manifest rapacity: the baby – her bright blue eyes, clamped shut – sucking tirelessly on anything offered. How, in fact, Marguerite St Chamas had returned, just as quickly as she could, to her function as not merely *la patrona* of that vast estate, but *lo patron*, as well.

Fallows then read his own, detailed description of how Guido, from the moment of the baby's arrival at that sprawling *bastide*, had become – if not her true father – an ideal substitute. Whenever he possibly could (on Sundays, for instance) he'd dote on the child. He'd wash himself down, plunging his arms – as far as his elbows – into a barrel of water, left alongside the *pigeonnier* for exactly that purpose. He'd then cross the flagstone courtyard to the baby carriage itself, standing in the deep shade of the tall, overhead hayloft. The carriage, wrapped in so much billowing gauze, looked as fluffy, as weightless – in that shade – as a giant meringue. Once there, Guido never so much as touched the child. He whispered, instead. He spoke softly through the gauze, telling the baby things that only the two of them might hear. He'd speak as through a screen, muttering small endearments, tiny confessions. Humming lullabies, as well. For Guido Stampelli, it would be as close as he'd ever come to having a child himself.

The mistral, just then, blew through the hotel bedroom. And Fallows – in the same moment – realized that this was the very wind that had blown, once, through that courtyard. Had billowed in the netting of the baby carriage, as – just now – it lifted the corners of the curtains, rose through the folds of Frédérique's shawl. She'd left her shawl hanging from a door handle. And now, with the wind, the peacocks printed across its surface seemed – for an instant – to flutter. To flutter then settle, lazily, amongst its emerald-green branches.

Fallows looked across at Frédérique sleeping: at the line of her cheek as it met the delicate crush of her pillowcase. He, too, might have found himself whispering – just then – to that sleeping figure. Muttering small endearments. After a moment, though, he returned to his manuscript. Returned to a long, rather intimate passage touching on Guido's relationship with Marguerite St Chamas. For Marguerite – it would appear – wanted more. Wanted what Guido could only assume to mean: more masonry. To double his productivity by carving, transporting, laying four stones a day, now, instead of merely two. Guido – as might be expected – hadn't the choice.

He moved, first of all, into the pigeonnier *itself*, Guy Fallows began reading, silently, to himself. He sat, now, no more than an arm's length from Frédérique's sleeping figure. *Moved into that lower of two rooms that had* served, in turn, as tool-shed, chicken coop, rabbit hutch, and – more recently – as a general débarras. He'd be saving rent thereby, and – just as precious – time he'd otherwise waste on needless displacements. So he brought along with him his few belongings, and draped them across the empty crates and broken harness chains, or hung them from the hulls of several, rusting ploughshares. And there, in the very midst of all that clutter, he'd sleep. Wrapped in a horse blanket that lay spread across a mattress of freshly cut straw, he'd sleep – in fact – in that tiny room throughout the autumn of 1945 and well into the winter of 1946. During that period, he'd work as he'd never worked in his life. Not only would he lay two stones, now, before daybreak, but two more – each day – after dark. After, that is, his own twelve-hour workday had terminated. He was clearly labouring at the very limits of the possible, putting in eighteen, uninterrupted work hours a day, now, nearly every day of the week.

Little, of course, would Guido suspect the real reason for that sudden precipitation. He'd go on assuming (as well he might) that Marguerite St Chamas simply wanted her pigeonnier completed that much earlier. He'd never know that her own proprietorial interests (the managing of her estate as well as the maintenance of the farm itself) had been superseded – for the first and only time of her life – by deeper needs. By those that, every twelve (rather than every twenty-four) days, now, would cause her mouth to draw open, and her lips to curl – round as the worn marble spout on the village fountainhead – into one of those boundless, boundlessly mute screams of hers.

No, Guido would never know this. Never even begin to suspect it. As to the fresh demands she'd just imposed, he'd accepted them in all innocence. Inwardly, of course, he could only feel joyous. He'd be able to visit that sombre

84

bedroom, now, so much the more. Make love to Marguerite St Chamas twice as often as he had. Despite all the added labour that that would entail, nothing – for Guido – could have made him happier. For now, he could climb that outer staircase, yes, every twelve days, the key's green ribbon – once again – lapping about the palm of his hand, then knock at that low, nail-larded door, as much out of fear (yes, even now) as simple respect. Once again, wait those four, five minutes (enjoying, perhaps, that state of self-inflicted anticipation) before using the key he'd been given – he could only assume – for his pleasure, and his alone.

Now within the dark, sparsely lit bedroom, he'd range his shoes, as always, one alongside the other, before climbing into that high, four-poster bed, and finding – under the grey coverlet and that heavy, taffeta skirt she still, needlessly, stubbornly insisted upon wearing – those plump buttocks, naked as his own.

'You make me work, my beauty, you certainly make me work,' Guido would whisper into the very midst of that piled, irresonant mass. For, over the months, he'd found the courage – bit by bit – to address her viva voce: to mutter 'little nothings' into the wilderness of her unbound hair.

'Like stars,' he once told her, haltingly. 'Each time, it's just . . .

'. . . just exactly like stars,' he resumed, catching his breath.

'. . . when the wind,' he continued. 'When the wind has washed the sky so clean that the stars . . .

'. . . that the little stars seem to flood the bigger ones,' he went on, more and more breathlessly, 'and you can't tell . . .

'. . . can't tell one constellation from another, there's so many . . .

85

'Oh, so many, so many stars, it's just like that. Like that,' he whispered – vehemently – into her ear. 'Oh, just like that . . .

'. . . like that . . .

'. . . like that,' he hissed, in extremis, *in the very same instant as his mouth slipped, wet, from her ear, and he rolled – exhausted – on to his back, his lips still moving, but silently, now. As silently, in fact, as those of Marguerite St Chamas.*

Two weeks later (two weeks, that is, after Guido had told Marguerite St Chamas all about the stars), she received a terse, four-word telegram, postmarked Tangiers.

'Arriving Friday,' it read, and was signed – quite succinctly – 'Emmanuel St Chamas'.

She read it over and over, incredulous. She kept reading and reading it, its brief message like some meat one has already tasted, even chewed, but cannot quite bring oneself to swallow. The boy who'd delivered it on a bicycle stood beside her, waiting for his tip, while Marguerite St Chamas went on reading and rereading the four-word telegram, incredulous.

9

There was no way of avoiding it, Guy knew. Solange
Daubigny had insisted on giving a rather sizable
reception for her daughter, Vic, and his son, Andrew.
It would, she felt, cast a certain respectability on to a
relationship that, in private, she could in no way approve
of. It would, at least, 'cover' the young couple locally: give
them a certain social cachet. And this, Solange Daubigny
felt, despite their decision. For Andrew and Vic had made
up their minds to leave: leave home, leave France, leave
Europe altogether. They wouldn't marry, they'd decided.
But no matter where they went, and no matter what
circumstances they might find themselves in, they'd sworn
to cherish and protect one another 'for ever and ever'.
Their vows, simply, wouldn't be public ones.

Solange Daubigny, of course, had hoped for a proper
marriage, *en bonne et due forme*. Having been denied that,
however, she'd chosen this rather aggrandized '*cocktail*',
instead. Her daughter had inherited a certain sum of
money from her father's father: she was legally an adult
and financially independent. As for Andrew, he'd saved
up a bit here, a bit there (nothing compared to Vic's
inheritance, of course), but enough to contribute to their
collective venture. No one, however, quite knew why
they'd chosen Patagonia to journey to. Not even, perhaps,

they themselves. They simply wanted to go – as they put it – as far as they could. Far as they could fly. As far from everything they'd ever known as was materially possible. 'Away', 'far away', was, in effect, their only destination.

The guests, that afternoon, had already gathered. They sat or stood about in the Daubignys' long, gracious living room, its walls flickering with early Provençal faience. The crowd was composed almost exclusively of local notables, successful either in business or in some branch of departmental politics. There wasn't, Guy Fallows noted, a single artist or intellectual present, only a rather loud, rather drunk dealer from an affluent gallery in Avignon. He was talking mostly in numbers. Fallows also remarked that virtually every man in the small crowd, aside from himself, was a hunter, and spoke of little else – that mid-summer afternoon – except the forthcoming *chasse*, that September. As for the women, nearly all of them wore pink: a high, saccharine, socially irreproachable pink.

'Tell me, Monsieur Fallows,' one of those women, seated opposite him in an overstuffed armchair, asked, 'do you ever die in any of your novels?'

'I'm sorry, I don't quite understand your question,' Fallows replied.

'Well, you know,' she went on, 'they say that if we dream our own death, we go on to live a very long, healthy life, indeed. I wonder if the same holds true in novels. If you write your own death, I mean, into any of your own books?'

'I wouldn't know,' Fallows replied somewhat dryly. 'I've never tried it.'

'Well, you *should*, you know,' the woman insisted, a bit giddy, no doubt, from too much champagne. 'A little death, once in a while, might do you some good. You know, in one of your books, I mean.'

She laughed all the more nervously, now, in response

to Fallows's apparent indifference. 'Just a *little* death, now and then,' she went on, irrepressibly. 'You'd see for yourself, it could make all the difference. I'm a reader, you know. I know about books. The fact that you write them doesn't qualify you as much as you'd think. Now, you listen to me,' she said, wagging a little, pink forefinger in Fallows's direction. 'Die a bit, once in a while. It will do you a power of good.'

Fallows walked to the far end of the long living room. He was looking – as he went – for Solange Daubigny. He felt a sudden, desperate need to find her. Instead, though, he ran into her husband, Maurice. 'Ah, there you are,' Daubigny exulted, 'my American novelist friend. How are you, old boy?' He was more jovial, now, than ever. Only four weeks remained – after all – before the first day of the hunt. Daubigny's spirits were up.

So, while Fallows stood there, trapped in conversation, his thoughts roamed down the long corridors and into the rooms of that spacious manor house, searching – as they went – for that lovely, all-too-tenuous creature.

'Come September,' Daubigny exulted, 'we'll get you whistling, don't think we won't. When you're out on walks, rest assured: you'll be whistling every song in your repertoire.'

'You *do* remember me, then,' Fallows answered, off-handedly.

'Remember you? The American novelist who doesn't hunt, how could I forget you? Furthermore, as of today, we're both somewhat related by this non-marriage we're celebrating, aren't we? We're nearly in-laws in a kind of non-legal way, don't you agree?'

While Daubigny went on talking, Fallows wondered if anyone had bothered to notice that the guests of honour – Vic and Andrew – hadn't yet arrived. Now that the reception, in fact, was well under way, it didn't seem to matter, either. Champagne vanished in one slender *tulipe* after another, and the general chatter had long since turned into so many outbursts of raucous laughter. Laughter, exclamation, and the gliding swoon of so much feigned compliment.

Fallows, at long last, found Solange Daubigny. She was combing out her short, blonde hair in front of a three-way vestibule mirror. What's more, she was quite by herself. Seated on a tall, embroidered settee, the line of her bare back took the slender, sinuous whip-curve of her vertebrae, while – at the same time – her chin, ever so slightly, rose in a gaze of ambivalent – if prolonged – self-regard.

Wordlessly, Fallows came up behind her. Running his arms about her shoulders, he cupped her breasts in each of his hands. They were taut, tumescent. Then, as if in counterpoint to his gesture, and virtually in the very same instant, she pivoted towards him, and slapped him firmly on one cheek, then the other. The unexpectedness of her reaction – almost certainly – hurt Fallows more than the slaps themselves.

'Never do that again, do you understand? Never,' she said in a heated whisper. Then rose, walked past him, and left the vestibule altogether.

Fallows found himself staring down into his open hands. They were still cupped as if to receive the contours of Solange Daubigny's small, swollen breasts. His hands lay, face up, and stared back at him like the imprints – they virtually were – of that vanished form.

There was nothing Fallows could do, now, but leave. He left quickly, discreetly. No one would have noticed his departure, either, in that crowded room where one conversation seemed a near-perfect duplication of the next. Where even the lives of those gathered were so totally interchangeable. Outside, in the early evening air, Fallows followed a crescent of black cypresses down to the parking lot, and there, almost immediately, ran into Vic and Andrew. They had just arrived.

'How's the party going, Guy?' Vic asked him. She was, as ever, dressed entirely in black. And her hair – once again – was so black it appeared blue: the blue of so much tempered steel.

He forced a smile. 'Pretty much as you might expect,' he answered, standing now, alongside his car.

'So we're not missing a single thing, right?' she asked. Her English was perfect, even colloquial.

'No,' he assured her, 'not a single thing.' She placed a hand on Guy Fallows's shoulder in a gesture of unspoken understanding. Fallows – for his part – liked Vic. He liked her chic, her independence. Most of all, he liked it that she and Andrew were going to live together. Travel together. Leave Europe entirely, and explore for themselves one of the very last, untrammelled reaches on earth. Yes, he thought, that together they'd both go 'far as they could fly'. Far as they could from these spent cultures. These exhausted societies. From those who went on living – pretending to live – off a world, inwardly depleted.

'Enjoy yourselves,' he told them, his hand on the door handle of his car.

Vic, on tiptoes, kissed Guy Fallows on the forehead. Unlike her mother – Fallows noted – she cast about her a somewhat cool, metallic scent, such as young women, then, were wearing.

'It's getting late,' he said gently. 'You two better be moving along.'

'In fact,' his son joined in, 'what time *is* it?' Andrew never wore a watch, and his relationship with time didn't differ altogether that much from his relationship with language. He tended – to the extent one could – to avoid it.

'It's nearly seven,' his father replied. 'You'd both, in fact, better get started.' And so they did. They kissed

Fallows on each cheek – *à la française* – then headed up the cypress-lined walk to the manor house itself.

Fallows, now, driving home, couldn't help thinking how right – yes, how terribly right – they were. It was nearly dark, now, and out of the corner of his eye, he could just distinguish the vine-rows speeding evenly past like the flicked pages of some unending book. Yes, he thought – kept thinking – as the pages turned faster and faster: how terribly right. And if Andrew, like so many young people today, could only express himself in a succession of vaporous phrases, perhaps – Fallows thought – the very vapour of those phrases surrounded something altogether unforeseeable. Was no less than the milk, for instance, enveloping the embryo of some yet undisclosed vision. One that Fallows himself couldn't in any way measure.

Yes, so right. So terribly right, he kept thinking, all the way to his house. The house itself lay perched on a rock outcropping, high over several terraced orchards of fruit trees. The leaves of the trees (mostly apricot) hung from the thick parasol of their branches like so many long, golden tongues. In the late light of twilight, they seemed aglow, while the stone house – just over them – stood crouched, brooding, unlit.

10

E^{*ven from there – from across the square – he could*} already hear them. Hear the boules *thudding dully against the dry ground, or clicking percussive – one against the other – in so many neat, deliberate collisions. Yes, even from there, from the shade of so much heavy, overhanging acacia, he must have watched them, too. Watched Guido, first of all, in a small circle of workmen, playing – that Sunday – four to a group. Must have seen how the peasants, mostly in blue, had formed into separate circles of their own, as had the artisans in their wide, wide-visored* casquettes. *How, in yet others, the shopkeepers – the* petite bourgeoisie – *stood playing or simply chatting in small, dusty clusters, dressed in waistcoats and watch chains, and in pinched, pearl-grey fedoras.*

How each of these circles, however, obeyed the exact same rules: those in which entire rounds of ice-cold pastis could be won or lost depending on the lay of a single boule, *the* boule *tape-measured to the least, thumb-bitten fraction of a single centimetre.*

From where he stood, he must have gone on watching. Gone on surveying the whole spectacle in general, and Guido in particular. Must have followed it all through the thin, recurrent veil of his own cigar smoke. That haze which – transparent – seemed to envelop the iron-grey stubble of his short, unshaved head. Rhythmically, he'd draw his cheeks to a hollow, squinting – as he did – through his narrow, acid-blue eyes at the village square, beyond. He probably went on watching, observing, scrutinizing that square for a considerable amount of time, in fact, before making his move. Must have heard their brief, exclamatory calls: the 'coquins de sòrt' and 'putaings' that punctuated, as each Sunday, that bright, dusty terrain. Heard, now – as he approached – those very same voices as if recede, fall silent, one after another. Must have seen, as he crossed the square, now, and came under the very same trees as they themselves, how – one at a time – their backs turned. How, like life-size dummies in a shooting gallery, they pivoted (but slowly, without the least trace of precipitation) to form, finally, a solid rampart of backs. A wall – casual as it was resolute – of collective rejection.

He kept coming, though, his tight boots scuffing the dust as he approached. He must have known, too, exactly what he wanted, for just as he came alongside that closed circle in which Guido Stampelli stood (murmuring along with the others), he stopped. He stopped, and slowly (perhaps no faster than the speed at which their backs had turned upon his approach) relit the ash-flaked stub of his cigar. Having done so, he stood now, blowing iron-grey aureoles of smoke about his unshaved head, and – with his cheeks sucked hollow – waited.

He might, of course, have gone directly to Guido's house, instead. Might have 'settled his business' there, in that tiny, unfurnished room that Guido, once again, had rented. But he hadn't dared. He was continuously on the qui-vive, now. On the alert. Anything that resembled a secluded space, a dark corridor, let alone someone's private lodgings, was – he well knew – to be avoided at all costs. For, curiously enough, he'd only been seen, since his return, in public: standing about, or sipping a bock – *quite by himself – at the village café. He wouldn't venture, either, very far from those groups, those informal gatherings that inadvertently – by their very numbers – protected him. Because any individual, from any one of those gatherings, taken separately, and given a location solitary enough, would – without an instant's hesitation – have gunned him down.*

As for Guido, his life had radically changed. He'd not only moved out of the pigeonnier *on the very day that telegram had arrived from Tangiers, but had stopped work on the dovecote altogether. For how could he possibly justify his presence? His unsalaried, unremunerated presence at that sprawling, rose stucco farmhouse? Hadn't Marguerite St Chamas been left penniless in the midst of what was – after all – a world war? What wages, then, had he worked for? And – without wages – how could he possibly explain a full year's gratuitous labour? What's more, how would* she *explain it, Guido kept asking himself, over and over, alone in his little bedroom with only a single, dangling light bulb for décor?*

But, once again, Marguerite St Chamas was well ahead of anything that anyone might possibly expect, let alone foresee. For on the very day that that telegram had arrived from Tangiers, she went about accomplishing two, quite separate tasks: namely, she buried a ring, and purchased a ledger: a tall, finely ruled livre de comptes. *First, she wrapped the ring (a rather sizable star sapphire she'd inherited from her mother, and which, with time, had taken on considerable value) in several sheets of tissue paper. Then, stuffing this into a small, silk purse, she buried its precious contents directly beneath a particular flagstone under her dining-room table. It was there, just there, that – at mealtimes, three times a day, every day of the week – she posed the tips of her two, surprisingly dainty, black shoes.*

This hadn't been easy. She'd barely managed, in fact, to pry the flagstone loose with the aid of a crowbar. Propping it – momentarily – against a wood block, she'd scooped out just enough earth to insert – and snugly – the bulging little purse, and, within it, the blue jewel itself. Then, having laid the heavy, grey flagstone back into position, she took her habitual place at the long dining-room table. It would be, in sorts, a kind of test. For there, with her somewhat plump calves tapering to a pair of slender ankles, she tapped the stone (or, rather, her secret, hidden just beneath it) with – yes – the very tip of her black shoes. Sitting there, now – her toes just touching the flagstone – the smallest of smiles escaped that normally tight, parsimonious, heart-shaped mouth of hers. Indeed, she even – for once – appeared pleased.

As for the ledger, she'd purchased it that very morning in Apt. And, as soon as she'd returned to her sprawling, rose stucco farmhouse, she'd immediately begun filling its pages with figures. With fictive accounts. Down its tall columns, page after page, she inscribed – in so many round, graceful loops – words on one side, numbers on another. The words referred to work executed – week after week, stone after stone – in view of the dovecote's total reconstruction. Whereas the numbers to the right indicated the exact sums (down to the last centime*) disbursed – for each of those labours – to 'the said stone-mason, Stampelli, G.'*

Peine perdue. For Emmanuel St Chamas returned to the farmhouse a broken man. Contrite, and fearing each instant for his life, he neither expected an accounting from his spouse, nor offered one himself. For clearly, he had none to offer. Not only had he emptied out their joint account, then fled, but worse – far worse – he had been responsible for the summary execution of twelve adolescents at the hands of the Nazis. No, he could neither offer nor expect anything now, except – almost certainly (but within how

many days, weeks, months?) – his own assassination. So,
as he stood there in the farmhouse doorway, that first
morning, a crushed hat in one hand and a satchel in the
other, Marguerite St Chamas – immediately – comprehended
this. And, in the very same instant, understood that all
the trouble she'd taken in burying the ring and buying
the ledger had been, in fact, utterly unnecessary. That
Emmanuel St Chamas was – and would remain, now –
entirely at her mercy.

She wasted no time, either. On the very day of his arrival,
after he'd unpacked his meagre belongings and made a few,
half-hearted gestures in the direction of his 14-month-old
daughter, she commenced. She hastily scribbled out the
first of several messages.

'I want work on the pigeonnier *resumed. Resumed*
immediately, do you understand?'

'On what, though, Marguerite?' he replied, careful to
make his words as legible as possible upon his moving
lips. 'With what could we pay a day-labourer,' he asked,
'let alone a stone-mason?'

'That's your problem, not mine,' she scribbled. 'It's you
who emptied out all our savings. Who left me penniless in
the midst of an armed occupation. It's up to you, not me,
to find the means.'

Then he, speaking. 'What about selling off some small
parcel of land? Like the meadow where we used to cultivate
oats? What about that, my Marguerite?'

Then she, scribbling, 'Out of the question.'

Then he, once again (but somewhat equivocally, now),
'There's the grape harvest, too. What about using part of
our profits, this year, from the coming grape harvest? We
could, you know.'

'We?' she dashed off, furiously, underlining the word
and the question mark three times.

'Well, whomever,' he deferred.

'We?' *she insisted, her handwriting gone wild, livid now, with indignation.*

'Then,' *he hesitated,* 'whatever profits . . . whatever profits you might make, ma Marguerite. From the grape harvest, whatever you might decide to do with the benefits.'

Emmanuel St Chamas might have heard – that very moment – a slight exhalation issue from his wife's lips. Seen, about the level of her bodice, a scarcely perceptible release. For Marguerite St Chamas had just that instant made her point, and her point – from then on – would be all-determinant.

'Get him,' *she wrote out, calmly as she could.* 'Get the stone-mason. I want work resumed immediately, do you understand?'

'But what can I offer him? In way of payment, what shall I say?'

'Offer him,' *she wrote out, as simply as that,* 'anything you're prepared to surrender. Anything,' *she continued in her long, steady, unperturbed script,* 'anything whatsoever. But get him.'

'With what, though?' *St Chamas pleaded.*

'You've spent everything there was to spend, exhausted every resource available,' *she wrote.* 'Now, why don't you use up whatever's left – if anything – of your own honour.'

'Honour?'

'Honour.'

'What are you asking, Marguerite? What are you asking me to do?'

'Spend it. Spend it, as well. It's a kind of currency, you know. A kind of resource of its own. You're good at spending, spend that – your honour – as well,' *she went on writing, with that ease – that newly acquired equanimity – that showed, now, with every stroke of her pen.*

'But in exchange for what?' St Chamas insisted.

Utterly placid, now, Marguerite St Chamas gazed across at her husband. He'd probably – in fact – never before seen that expression upon her face. 'In exchange,' she wrote out in so many tall, graceful loops, 'for the one thing you still think you possess.'

That night, Marguerite St Chamas unearthed her star sapphire. Once again, she'd prised the ungainly, grey flagstone loose with a crowbar, then recuperated – in its shimmering silk purse – her smothered ring. She slipped it on to her finger, now, and – in crossing the dark dining-room floor – thought of Guido with growing intensity. Of Guido's breath. Of his lips, toying with her earlobes, and his thighs pressed hard, relentless, against her own buttocks. Yes, she thought of Guido as she took the narrow staircase, now, to her bedroom, the thin pencil-line of her eyebrows arched high, and an expression – serene as it was seignorial – drawn as if permanently across the full surface of her face.

The boule *went blue as it rose. Reflected, against its metallic flanks, the very light – very air – it rose through, powered thus by the arm, the fingers, by the flicked wrist upwards. Reaching, now, the apogee of its arc, it seemed – for the briefest instant – to pause. As if to hang – in mid-air – weightless. To shimmer, now, even bluer than before. Then, gathering rapidly back into so much mass (no longer the object of its own release, but a body subject – like any other – to gravitational forces), it entered its own, predetermined descent. Went, as it plummeted, from sky-blue to burnt sienna. Yes, already reflected the oncoming earth, the ground with which – an instant later – the* boule *– in a puff of dust – would collide.*

'Bien joué,' *the voice, just behind Guido, remarked. 'I couldn't have played that shot any better myself,' it* said.

99

The boule *had just rolled into a bright puddle of* boules, *and was still clicking, now, quietly amongst them.*

Guido *pretended not to hear. Not to notice. So, too, did the other three players, standing about their twelve, played-out shots. They began measuring the closest of these, now, against the jack, the wooden* cochonnet *that each of those shots had been aimed at.*

'Bien, très bien,' *the voice persisted. It punctuated each of its phrases with a quick, quivering wreath of cigar smoke.*

The others, their backs firmly turned, went on measuring the boules, *using – as ruler – the straightest twig available. Pinching the twig, now, between thumb and forefinger, one of the players marked the distances between the closest lying* boules *and their* cochonnet. *He went from one to the next, kneeling each time with the pinched twig in hand, resembling – as he did – a kind of officiant in some primitive ritual.*

'It's the *boule just to the right,' the voice proffered. 'That one, just there,' it pointed. And, sure enough, it was. But the four players feigned to ignore this. Went on measuring the* boules *with the meticulousness of those whose livelihood had always depended on eyeing wood, or stone, or wrought iron, down to a perfect flush.*

'To the right, I'm telling you. That one, just there,' *the voice insisted, its words wrapped in so many loose corkscrews of smoke.*

The voice, in itself, had no power whatsoever, except – perhaps – the power to repel. Not violently, but with the steady, insidious effect – say – of some obnoxious odour. Or the rumour of some incurable disease that sends people, instinctively, into so much self-protective quarantine. So it was with the players. They kept away. They kept away from those empty utterances as they would, in effect, from the disease itself.

But the voice (the voice enveloped in its corkscrews of smoke) was indefatigable. It went on offering suggestions, advice, addressing the players' backs with whatever trite little pointers it could to shatter that tight circle they stood in. To create a breach in its midst. In that round of casquettes that – wide as pies – seemed to tilt, in a geometry of their own, towards the clustered boule balls, beneath.

And, what's more, it worked. Operating as a repellent, it wasn't so much the voice itself as its very presence – its sheer proximity – that brought one player, then another, to break – discreetly as they could – from that closed circle. They left to join other circles, other clusters, playing in the dappled shade of the same, dusty square. At a certain distance, now, they stood about – indistinguishable from the others – their arms pendant and their palms as if swollen with those fat, metal spheres. They'd entered, already, another game.

Only two, now, remained. Isolated, they appeared to be playing out of pure habit, waiting for the moment – the pretext – to end the game altogether, and be gone. To get as far as they could from that very area, which – by the presence of the third (its voice, as ever, wrapped in the volutes of so much cigar smoke) – had become thoroughly contaminated.

'If you knock the boule out just to the left,' the voice proffered, 'you'll have won the whole match. You'll see. You'll see for yourself, if you do what I tell you.' Once again, its words fell, if not unnoticed, at least unheeded. They'd as if dissolve in the ambient shade where the players' dull, ongoing murmurs were punctuated – here and there – by the sharp, irrecusable clicks of so much tossed and now neatly colliding metal.

'To the left, just to the left, Stampelli,' the voice as if commanded. And Guido, by the mere mention of his name, felt implicated, even infected by whatever contagion that voice happened to be propagating.

'There, just there,' it pointed out, impatiently.

Guido didn't answer. But the second player reacted almost immediately. With a quick set of murmured excuses, he moved off, joining the others on the far side of that same, earthbeaten terrain. Guido, now, was alone: alone with the voice. He gathered up his boules as slowly, casually, as he could, and, one after another, lobbed them into the air: into the leaf-shattered light. Then he watched them, one at a time, as they dropped, striking the ground in more or less the places – those narrow patches of dust – he'd intended. He was playing against no one, now, if not himself.

'I've got a message,' the voice confided, its words – as ever – twisted in smoke. 'I've got a message, and it's addressed to you,' it added, pointing the damp stub of its cigar in Guido's direction.

Guido, though, kept his back turned, and went on – as unperturbedly as before – tossing boules into that shattered light. It was, he might have thought, a bit like casting lots, or rolling dice, seeing which way the boules happened to fall. Which way, finally, they'd lie.

'It's from Madame,' the voice resumed, breaking through so much iron-grey bristle. 'It's from Madame, and it's addressed to you, Stampelli. Do you hear, it's for you, Stampelli.'

Guido put an extra spin on the next shot he lobbed, so that, in landing, the boule would as if counter its own thrust. Would – as it touched ground – rotate in place, digging a minuscule nest for itself within the powdered dust.

'Well?' the voice exclaimed, angered by the absence of any response whatsoever. 'Who's going to read it, Stampelli, huh? You or me?'

102

Guido remained perfectly silent. He squinted out towards the last boule he'd lobbed, his eyes and half his nose as if cropped by the shadow that fell, in a heavy crescent, from his visor downwards.

'Well, have it your way, then,' the voice, in response to nothing, retorted. And, as it did, its hand reached into the canvas pocket of a hunting jacket, and pulled out the message. Pulled out that tiny, unmistakable, twice-folded square that blossomed – as it broke open between ten, stub-like fingers – into an equally unmistakable calyx of cornflower blue.

'Have it your own way, then,' the voice repeated, and began reading the message, that missive it held – taut – in each hand.

'Resume,' it read. 'I want you to resume, resume immediately, do you understand? There are no obstructions, either. Perfectly none. I'm expecting you now, this week, immédiatement, is that clear? Marguerite St Chamas.'

The voice that had delivered the message folded it back, now, into that same, tiny square it had sprouted from. But Guido wasn't watching. He was in the process of calculating the yet invisible trajectory his boule had to take. He needed to eliminate a previous shot, lying in the dust like an obstacle, so many metres before him. He'd aim low, he decided, and attempt to knock one boule out with another in what's called, in those parts, un carreau sur place.

With his arm, from wrist to shoulder, held stiffly as a single, inflexible limb, he swung it from under, and sent the steel ball flying. Never more than half a metre from the ground, and travelling fast as an automobile, it struck the second boule squarely, causing it to bound – in two, three leaps – like a shot rabbit that sprints, for an instant, on reflex alone, then expires. So it was with the boule.

The second had replaced the first, and lay, now, in the sun, not only lambent but gathering light – it would seem – as it did. Guido, his arm limp, his hand empty, stood there and watched it. Watched it as if glimmer.

The baker – once again – was the first to know. Because exactly three days later, he heard the thumping of that very same wheelbarrow over cobbles, and – along with it – the knocking of one stone against another as the wheelbarrow came down through the dark village from the quarry above, and headed towards the plains, just beyond. Three kilometres across those very plains stood the sprawling, rose stucco farmhouse, its rooftops, at that hour, still as if encrusted with stars. And, alongside the farmhouse, the pigeonnier *itself in a cage of scaffolds. Once again, it was under construction.*

11

S he never even mentioned it. It was as if the reception, the
episode in the vestibule, the slaps she'd handed Fallows
before her three-way mirror, had never happened. Had
nothing, in any case, to do with *her* life. With Frédérique's,
that is.

When she telephoned Fallows several days later, her
mood – on the contrary – was perfectly ebullient. She
wanted to 'celebrate', as she put it. In fact, the whole
idea of having lunch in public – under the white, oblong
umbrellas at Le Bistrot à Michel – was entirely hers. So,
too, was her willingness, as Guy Fallows noted, to risk
so much exposure, for at the Bistrot, even in August, the
'smart set' converge, those with the gorgeous farmhouses
converted – with unfailing attention and unlimited funds
– into so much elegant shell. Into so many spaces gutted
– for décor's sake – of any functional aspects whatsoever.
Yes, 'they' were there. But none whom either Frédérique
or Guy recognized. So, indeed, through the long lunch, the
two of them felt free to 'celebrate', washing down their
filets de rouget au safran with one frosted goblet of *rosé*
after another.

They had nearly finished their second bottle of Tavel,
in fact, when the trouble started. Guy – almost certainly
– had sensed it coming. Because Frédérique, during the

past quarter hour, had begun – ever so slightly – slurring her words. Eliding, occasionally, a syllable here, a syllable there. For Guy, this served as an early – yet infallible – warning. As a storm flag, of sorts.

'It's such a pity, don't you find?' she asked in that wet, somewhat slippery diction she'd fallen into. 'Such a terrible, terrible pity, don't you agree?'

Guy didn't answer. He watched her beautiful gaze rise up to meet his, and once again noticed those immensely long lashes. Compared them, once again, to marine cilia. Or some tiny, involuted frond that a tropical botanist might have risked his life for. But this time, there was something turbid – disturbed – as her gaze came to meet his. She wasn't smiling, either.

'Well? Isn't it? Isn't it a pity?'

'What, my love?' he asked gently. He was trying to determine – behind the lovely, luminous veil of her *regard* – the source of that growing turbulence. The electricity he sensed gathering behind so much uninterrupted blue.

'I think it's such a pity,' she resumed, 'such a terrible pity that you're not – what's the word – "omniscient". Yes, that's it, "omniscient".'

She took a long sip of wine. As she did, Fallows noted how her cheeks – bathed in the *rosé*'s round, wobbling reflection – flushed even deeper. When she looked up, however, over the rim of her glass, her gaze – suddenly – had gone distant. Diffuse. She looked at Fallows, now, as at a stranger, the lines about her eyes deeply furrowed.

'Such a pity,' she continued. 'Yes, such a terrible, terrible shame. Oh, there are *so* many things you ought to know, and simply don't. Oh, *so* many things.'

'Such as what?' he asked, gently as before.

'Such as *everything*,' she responded. That tight knot of glances – complicities – that they'd known, had come, now, totally undone. 'Such as the stars, for instance,' she resumed, a bit giddily, slurring her words as she went. 'Such as the names of the stars. *All* the stars,' she added, with a sweeping motion of one hand. 'Oh, how I'd love to be in love with a man who knew the name of each and every star. Oh, how I'd love that,' she said, her voice dropping off into a small, private sigh of its own. She sat there, now, thoroughly self-absorbed.

Then, redressing herself, she asked, somewhat peevishly, 'But you *don't*, do you. You *don't* know each and every star.'

He didn't answer.

'It's not only the stars, either,' she went on, 'it's all kinds of things. *All* kinds,' she repeated.

Fallows remained silent.

'Take the mushrooms, for instance. You ought to know everything – simply everything – about mushrooms, for instance. But you don't, do you. You really don't,' she added with growing irritation. 'Nor the lichens, either. The little red lichens, for instance. Nor the frogs that croak and croak and croak on summer nights, while you sit there listening, not knowing a single, blessed thing about their gizzards or their oesophagi or whatever it is that allows them to croak as they do. No, not a single, blessed thing.

'But there's worse,' she said, pouring herself a glass of wine from the near-empty bottle, then gesturing to the waiter for yet another.

'Why don't we order coffee, instead?' Fallows suggested.

'Because there's worse, much worse, that's why,' she went on, leaning back now in her straw armchair, an arm draped against its high, lacquered frame. 'About the stars, you see, I can understand. That you don't know a blessed thing about the stars, or the mushrooms, or the frogs, all of that – for instance – I can accept. But there's something

107

worse, much worse,' she promised, as the waiter filled her glass, then Guy's, with wine from a fresh, freshly chilled bottle. Filled it with that icy, pink vintage that contained (as Fallows might well have recognized) the distilled memory of other summers. Of so much wind and shadow. Of light – in bright gusts – sweeping through the umbrellaed terraces of other restaurants where yet other couples, once, had reached impasses of their own.

'What is it?' Fallows asked. 'What is it, *ma bien-aimée?*'

'This,' she said, placing her spread fingers against the flat of her breast. 'Just here,' she said with sudden calm.

'What, though?' he insisted.

'Just here, just this,' she said.

'*Dis-moi. Dis-moi, je t'en prie.*'

'It's where . . .' she began, 'just where I felt absolutely certain that you knew everything. Everything about Frédérique. Every thought, every feeling, every tiny little sensation, here, just here,' she said, the tips of her fingers fanning delicately now across her chest, reaching – as they went – towards the long, slender line of her bare collarbones. 'Here, just here,' she said.

Fallows tried to take her other hand into his, but she withdrew it. Then, shaking her head, she whispered to no one, now, except herself, 'Hate it, how I hate it, oh God, how I hate it, hate it that you're not God.' Then, looking up, suddenly, into his eyes with an expression that was both perfectly childlike, and – at the same time – immensely, immeasurably archaic, she asked, 'Because you aren't, are you?'

Fallows remained perfectly silent. He emptied out his wine glass, then poured himself another: filled it, quivering, to the brim. As he did, he listened – with a kind of refracted attention – to the sounds that arose from the tables about them: the clatter of glassware and china that seemed to envelop the light exchange of so many strange voices like fronds about a single, ephemeral flower.

'Because you really, really, really aren't, are you? Aren't God. Aren't anything but another lover. Oh, how I hate it. Hate it. Hate it that you're nothing more than another lover,' she went on, shaking her head, and muttering to herself in a mantra of her own making: 'Not God, not God, not God, oh how I hate it that you're not God.'

Frédérique, as Fallows well knew, was not only thoroughly drunk, but deeply depressed. Somewhere, though, in the midst of so much wild declaration, she was expressing – in hopelessly hyperbolic terms – her own, heartfelt truth. Of this, he was well aware. She had expected from their relationship something 'other', elevated, even – perhaps – transcendent. Had expected (he knew) more than he could have ever given. More, probably, than *anyone* could have ever given. Had anticipated, from their passion, something all-surpassing. Yes, a rapture, of sorts.

This, in fact, hadn't been the only time that Guy Fallows had been confronted with the incommensurability of a woman's expectations. Nor – it could be said – with the paucity of a man's responses. It was a situation – a human cosmogony, in a sense – with which he was all too familiar. What he'd never understood, however, and still couldn't fathom, were the reasons for – the causes of – those insuperable differences. What kept a woman pleading, in a particular relationship, for *something so much more*, where a man – any man – in an equivalent situation, would simply acquiesce. Settle for whatever he had. Or, in default of that, go adrift: move from one mate to the next in what, finally, was nothing other, in fact, than a kind of serial – sequential – acquiescence. Asking, as he went, not so much from any one, particular woman, as from an image he coveted of all women (with everything

109

that implied of endless replacement, myriad replication), what a woman would ask – even beg – only from a single, exclusive presence: that of the beloved himself. That which knew no substitutes.

Failing this, she in her need (in the need that rose only higher with each successive deception) would begin beating on walls, while he – at the exact same moment – packed his bags. Made reservations on the very next flight. Travelled across the entire surface of the earth – acquiring this, divesting himself of that – yet never really settling, 'in body and spirit', anywhere. Never dwelling within any particular love for longer than it took to exhaust its possibilities as image, idea. As some form of psychic idyll. As something – that is – it never was.

And so, Fallows thought, we wander, don't we. For it's us, the exiles, he continued. Us, the strangers, here. Always outside, looking in. Moving, as we do, from one illusory relationship to another. From one scent to the next. Yes, from honeysuckle to honeysuckle. While they: they're as if caught, caught from within. Ballasted in a flesh that's never been anything other than itself: than the woman, who – self-perpetuating – crouches within the woman. And begs, begs – as she does – for release.

Wasn't it this, Fallows continued, that they sought? Some kind of deliverance? Sought the 'God', the 'demiurge', the force capable of pulling – from their very innards – that hidden self? That double? Delivering them – by some forceful yet subtle act of obstetrics – of that *something so much more*? That 'other' in whom – at long last – they might entirely recognize themselves? And, in so doing, come free?

Fallows had not only named Frédérique, he'd drawn her – to the extent that he could – out of so much bourgeois sterility. The pseudonym – in a sense – had given her a place to flee to. And, thanks to this, the two of them had been able to come together, each Thursday, in that passionate *commedia* of their own making. Over and over, had been able to create – out of their own fingers and teeth, out of the steady abrasion of their own flesh – a heat, an immediacy, a profound complicity such as neither of them had ever known.

Frédérique, however, wanted more. Wanted to be drawn, it seemed, into some carnal heaven from which she'd never return. Wanted to be absolved – Fallows realized – of all memory, all past. Yes, delivered. At long last, delivered. A god, a god, indeed, Fallows thought to himself. No wonder Frédérique berated him for not being a god.

'It's as much as I can do,' he said, suddenly. 'From day to day, as far as I can take it.'

'I'm afraid,' she whispered.

'It's what there is, my beloved,' he answered. 'It's already so much. So very, very much.'

'I'm afraid,' she whispered, perfectly sober, now. 'I'm afraid for Frédérique. Afraid we're going to lose her. Both of us, lose her.' She faced sideways as she spoke, enunciating each word, now, with a kind of halting precision. Her entire profile, from the gold blade of her hair to her perfectly chiselled, perfectly proportioned features, reminded Fallows – that very instant – of an amber intaglio. It moved him to the very quick.

'Don't lose her,' she whispered, still facing sideways across the heavily shaded terrace.

Fallows took her hand between both of his, and mar- velled – as always – at its extreme slenderness.

'Don't let her simply dissolve,' she pleaded. 'Simply vanish.'

He rubbed his thumb – deep – across the cupped hollow of her palm, and assured her that he wouldn't. 'Of course, I won't,' he told her. In the very same instant, though, Fallows realized that there was nothing he could do, either, to hold Frédérique. To keep her from dissolving, as she'd put it. In a way, hadn't the process already begun? At some point, he sensed, hadn't the extravagant theatre they'd created for themselves those past few months lost its delicate underpinnings? The tenuous ground on which it stood? Hadn't Frédérique – as an entity – begun dissolving already? Vanishing into something as insubstantial – as arbitrary – as that choice of names out of which she'd first emerged?

Fallows ran his thumb, now, even deeper into the very heart of her palm. 'Let's go,' he said, suddenly.

'Yes,' she said, turning towards him. 'Let's.'

'Now, right now,' he pleaded.

'Yes,' she said, bringing a pink napkin up to the corner of her lips. 'Yes, yes,' she said, almost solemnly. 'Right now.'

He pulled his thumb free from her hand, and gestured in the direction of the waiter. As he did, a gust of wind blew through the terrace, billowing – overhead – in the buff-white, oblong umbrella. The ribs of the umbrella, in the very same instant, rattled.

But it didn't work. The two of them – that afternoon – as soon as the door of their hotel bedroom was bolted and the curtains pulled, stripped as quickly – silently – as they could. Then, together, they took to the bed's stiff, overlapping linen with a kind of parched desperation. Rising to his every thrust, retracting – rhythmic – to his every retraction, Frédérique – nonetheless – wasn't 'there'. Much as Fallows might have tried to awaken her to herself, she simply wasn't present. Her body, though, went through the whole, burgeoning ritual of it all. Even climaxed – somewhat dolorously – in the very same moment as Fallows himself. Still, that persona, that image, that role in which she'd come to recognize herself,

112

were all curiously absent, that afternoon. For all intents and purposes, Guy Fallows had just, in fact, copulated with a perfect stranger.

He looked across at her closed eyelids, now; with stress, the wrinkles at their very edges had become all the more apparent. He'd failed her, he knew. But he'd failed her – he went on thinking – at some quasi-metaphysical level. Some dizzying altitude of the spirit – or the imagination – to which he'd never claimed to have knowledge, let alone access.

He went on thinking these things, as he lay alongside her, now, staring up into the room's cool, cloistered darkness. As Frédérique slept, he thought of those 'heavens', those high, hallucinatory spaces that no one, really, acceded to. That nothing did, but the heart, the heart's insistence. Its terrible pounding.

When, a full hour later, she awoke, she scarcely seemed to recognize him. He watched her as she rose, then slowly began dressing. She did so as if Fallows weren't even present. Didn't even exist. Then, as she pulled on the long, transparent sheath of her stockings, she said, as if to herself alone, 'It doesn't seem to happen any longer, does it?'

He didn't answer.

With one slender leg crossed over the knee of the other, she drew each stocking up to the height of her thigh. 'It doesn't, though, does it?' she went on. 'Simply doesn't, that's all. What else can one say?' Her voice had taken on that distant, disembodied quality that Fallows had first heard – months earlier – when Frédérique had spoken of her father. Had first evoked his memory.

She stood up, once again, and walked over to the tall wardrobe mirror. There, fully dressed, she tilted her head one way, then another, examining her reflection as – say –

a fashion designer might examine a mannequin. She didn't give the least sign, either, of recognizing herself.

'Oh, those clouds,' she exclaimed suddenly. 'Making love, do you remember them, those clouds? How golden they were? How perfectly golden?' she asked. She was in the process, just then, of arranging a few stray hairs with the very tip of her index fingers. The rest of her hands fanned upwards and out to form a rather sprightly pair of pronged, rose-coloured horns.

'Oh, how they scorched,' she went on, talking entirely to herself, now. 'Burnt to the very quick. Oh, remember? Remember how they burnt?' she went on, asking no one except herself, while Fallows – propped up against a single pillow – looked on. Watched her prepare herself, adjusting this, concealing that, and felt – as he did – as if he were witnessing his heart's own funeral.

'Of course,' he lied. 'Of course, I remember how golden they were. How terribly golden. And yes, how they scorched. Of course, of course I do,' he told her.

But she wasn't listening. Wasn't – for all intents and purposes – any longer present. She'd plunged half the length of her forearm into a deep, leather handbag, and could just detect, now, at the base of that bag, the faint jingle of her car keys. This seemed to please her. Or – at least – reassure her. She smiled as she heard the familiar jingle, but even her smile seemed directed at no one, not even herself.

12

There'd be the stones, he thought to himself.

There'd be the solid, hand-crafted blocks of his paragraphs, his chapters, his book. Yes, *The Pigeonnier*, he went on. There'd be the dovecote he was constructing for Frédérique every bit as patiently – lovingly – as Guido had constructed his, so many years earlier, for Marguerite St Chamas. Yes, there'd be the tower. The rigorous, mineral evocation of that space, that world, dealing – as it did – with her childhood. Yes, with her poor, obscured childhood.

Only the book, the book alone – Fallows felt convinced – could bring Frédérique back to herself. Yes, out of those vaporous immensities in which – week after week – she'd felt herself dissolving, only the book could serve as grounding. As root. As somewhere she might – in recognizing her own, lost identity – come to some kind of terms with herself. For, as Guy Fallows realized, in order to save their love, he had – first of all – to save Frédérique herself. Their *commedia*, he had to admit, had ended, now. Their fabulous Thursdays. For how, indeed, could the beautiful she-moth to whom he'd given the name Frédérique come entirely free of that first chrysalid? How could anyone – for that matter – without risking total dissolution? There weren't two realities, two truths. Weren't so many sets of interchangeable identities. No, he thought, but there were the stones, weren't there? The solidity of his narrative. His carefully constructed fiction which – in restoring her past – might serve indeed as a basis for some possible future. Even, perhaps, some possible life, together.

Yes, and realizing this, he returned to his manuscript, now, with an urgency such as he'd never before known. Yes, he returned to Guido, that very day, and to Marguerite St Chamas's sprawling, rose stucco farmhouse. How Guido, once again, had set up his scaffolds, laid out his planks, and resumed – stone after stone – the restoration of that handsome, sixteenth-century structure. In order to do so, Guido had had to abandon several commissioned projects: one, already underway, and two or three others in the offing. Yes, in answer to Emmanuel St Chamas's 'invitation', he had to give himself now, and throughout the summer and autumn of 1946, to the tower. The tower, alone. To its slow, steady accretion in blocks the colour of hay bales and a weight approaching that of his own. He worked all summer and autumn as he'd never worked before, not even during that arduous winter, two years earlier. With an intensity bordering on the demonic, he stopped for nothing all day, either, if not a quick *casse-croûte* (usually a half-loaf of bread and a dry slab of ham or marbled mortadèlla, along with a swig of water from a battered, tin thermos he carried – like keys – a bit everywhere). No, he'd stop for nothing now, except – occasionally – a drink, or quick bite, or – for a few minutes here and there – to play with the *patrona*'s little girl, Solange. For Solange had learnt to toddle, now. And, invariably, would make her way – with a few, harmless tumbles – to the work-site itself. A peasant girl would come scurrying out after her, but not before the little child had found Guido. Had wrapped her tiny arms about the calves of his blue, mortar-speckled trousers, and, in seemingly no time, the knees of those very same trousers

116

(gone, in the interim, that much paler). Yes, rushed to that 'almost father' to whom, from the very first, she was so inordinately attached.

The tower, as it went on rising, increasingly became – for Guido – a kind of testimonial, a declaration of sorts, of his love for Marguerite St Chamas. It was, as he called it, his *offerte*, his offering to that austere presence whose plump, curvaceous figure might well have reminded him of church paintings he'd seen in his early childhood: of those huge, baroque Virgins, who – brooding and forlorn – stared down on his young head out of so many dark, taper-lit chapels.

It took Guido, now, no more than eight days to complete a ring, a freshly laid course of limestone blocks, and earn – as he might have called it – his 'admission'. To recuperate the key with its dangling, green ribbon, and take – after having thoroughly bathed, shaved, and dressed to the hard starch of his collar – that stone staircase. And there, once again, knock. Yes, knock on that same, nail-larded door. Wait those four, five, insupportable minutes he'd impose upon himself (as much out of an abiding timidity as an unequivocal respect) in order to hear what – materially – he knew he'd never hear: her response. Then, the four, five minutes having elapsed, he'd turn the key – the green ribbon lapping, once again, over the edge of his hand – and enter.

Only this time, he didn't. He wouldn't. For here, the whole story of Guido, of Guido's love for Marguerite St Chamas, veers, goes askew. Like virtually everything else in Guy Fallows's narrative, this part of Guido's story originated in the still living rumours that circulated through that very same village. Those very same cafés. There where the elders – *lei vielhs* – were all too ready, between two games of *belote*, to confirm and elaborate upon each and

117

every incident. Inform Fallows – to the extent they could – of each particularity.

For Guido never again took to that staircase, they told him. Never again pleasured in the rolling hips and rich buttocks of *la Chamassa*, as they called her. He went on building, though. Went on erecting that tower in a kind of scarcely controlled fever, giving to the work at hand the kind of passion he might otherwise have given to her, and her alone. To what he still only knew (could only imagine) as the dispassionate mass of *la patrona* herself.

No, he'd stop for nothing, either, if not that occasional swig of water, or bite of stale sandwich; if not for that little girl who'd tug – from time to time – at his trousers, and beg to be swung, or shown the little birds'-nests that Guido, and Guido alone, would invariably discover, hidden in the prickly heart of the blue junipers. Occasionally, though, he'd catch sight of Marguerite St Chamas herself. She'd come to her window, overlooking the courtyard (it stood at the very same level as the now nearly completed *pigeonnier*). Once or twice, Guido felt fairly certain that Marguerite St Chamas had been trying to catch his attention, waving a bright scarf, or handkerchief. He'd pretend not to notice, though. He'd go on working. Or, rather, attempting to work. Attempting to appear as if he were still working. For, in fact, Marguerite St Chamas was all he ever thought of, throughout the day. All he ever dreamt of, longed for. His love – call it his 'adulation' – hadn't changed. If anything, it had deepened with each passing month. Now, though, he felt that he no longer needed, as before, to violate her very person. Cause her such affront. To bring his heated breath – still smelling, no doubt, of rabbit and woodsmoke – against the plump little corollas of her earlobes. No longer needed to shove, insist, ramming his swollen sex between those two, tightly pressed petals, before making his way into the dome of

118

that thoroughly impassive organ, plundering, plundering her, over and over, he felt, like a man gone wild.

All that – he'd decided – had ended for ever. He'd no longer subject that creature, whom he adored above all others (adored, and – he might have added – dreaded, as well), to such ignominy. No, despite her husband, and his base solicitations. And despite whatever signs she herself might have given from her bedroom window (Guido took them to mean: 'Go on, go on with your work, don't stop'), he'd spare her, now, the insult, the offensiveness of it all. No, she'd no longer need to debase herself. And he, he'd no longer need to receive (as she'd called it) his 'compensation'. It would be compensation enough, now, to complete the tower. Make of it his offering. To let it rise (as it would, soon enough) into a bouquet of fluttering, white pigeons.

And thus, all his love (and – it might be added – all his resources, as well: the meagre savings he'd managed to accumulate over the past half-year from other work-sites) was poured into the tower. Poured, that is, into that monument he was reconstituting for Marguerite St Chamas. For her, who'd still – from time to time – appear at her window, waving (rather forlornly, now) that bright scarf or handkerchief. And which Guido – all the while – would feign to ignore. He was working, he assured himself, as fast as he could.

'And all that, for love,' one of the card players in the local café jested to Guy Fallows, nearly a half-century later. He kept a spent cigarette in his mouth.

'For love,' he repeated, mockingly as before, as his eyes slipped – smooth – over a freshly dealt hand. The cards themselves, dark scarlet, glistened in the light that fanned, alluvial, on to the heads of the four players and the felt cloth of the card table, below. *'Per amor,'* he repeated in a tone as bitter as it was oblique, off-hand.

The card player, who was elderly, had known Guido as an adolescent. As such, he'd given Guy Fallows the clearest, first-hand image he had of that now nearly forgotten figure. That maker of dovecotes, whose blue work clothes – according to the old man – were white as a baker's from that bright cloud of stone dust he seemed permanently enveloped in.

The old man, now, picking up the eight, smooth playing cards he'd just dealt himself, inspected each, the cold butt of his cigarette still dangling from between his lips. 'For love,' he repeated, as bitterly as before. 'For the love of some bitch or another (*quauca salòpa o d'una autra*),' he murmured, staring down at his cards.

'For the love of some bitch or another,' the second player chimed in, 'man has built every dovecote on earth, you can rest assured. And every farm, every farmhouse, as well.'

'That's perfectly certain,' the third player, in that sombre chorus of card players, concurred. Then, raising the level of woman's cupidity yet one more degree, he added, 'And castles. Castles, too. For the love of some bitch, he's built every fortress, every walled city you've ever seen. There's no limit, either, that he hasn't gone to. No risk that he hasn't taken.'

'For love,' the first murmured, dealing out cards.

'For love,' the second repeated, as he gathered them up, then – with a single rub of his fat thumb – spread them into a tight, scarlet fan.

'*Si, per amor,*' sighed the third, as he flung out the first card, and initiated the game.

The fourth, who'd remained silent, was thinking to himself: 'Yes, for love. That's certain. Had written, too. For love alone, had written, written his books.' There was no bitterness, however, as he murmured these things. None whatsoever. Only – if anything – regret. 'And broken into houses, and held up armoured trucks, too,'

120

he thought, remembering – as he did – his favourite poet. 'For love, the whole thing. The whole, blessed, cursed, impossible thing,' he went on thinking (but not saying), as the cards got reshuffled, redealt, rearranged (between a thumb that deployed and a forefinger that cradled) in ever-recurrent combinations, immutable – he knew – as the fates themselves. And every bit as fixed as the stars.

'For love, for love,' he went on whispering to himself well after the game had finished, and the café closed. After he'd made his way home, and – once there – uncorked a fresh bottle of that pale, honey-coloured *marc*. Smelt its aroma rise – burnt, earthen – through his nostrils, flooding, as it did, his every cell.

'Yes, for love. For love, indeed,' he muttered.

13

'Wait, wait,' she'd say. Of that, he was perfectly certain.

'Wait, just another few weeks. Until it's finished, Guy. Yes, just as soon as it's finished,' she'd say, attempting, by every means possible, to delay that confrontation. That inevitable encounter with nothing less – in fact – than her lost self. Her own, absconded childhood. With that world that – stone after stone – *The Pigeonnier* had so patiently, lovingly, reconstituted.

But now, he knew, it wouldn't wait. Mustn't wait. For they'd arrived at that critical moment in which Frédérique (and, along with her, her love) would either dissolve with her own dissolving persona, or solidify. Gather about so much veritable image. Rediscover herself in those pages as in the heavy, black leaves of some long since forgotten family album. Yes, like that. Exactly like that. For there's no greater gift any of us can give one another, Fallows thought – that very moment – than the gift of a mirror. The reflection in which the other – the beloved, in this instance – might finally bathe.

Yes, bathe. For Frédérique (Fallows could scarcely call her by anything but that pseudonym) rarely, if ever, caught glimpses of herself. Even her name – her given name – was something, indeed, she'd never heard her own parents pronounce. Her mother, of course, had been mute. And her father – her detested father – had died, under somewhat mysterious circumstances, before her own memory could be said to have begun. No, her name – in a sense – had never been 'authenticated'. Had never rung through the rooms of her childhood, giving it – and herself, in turn – an identity of its own. And thus, that lifelong drift, Fallows realized. Thus, that continuous search, year after year, not merely for a new name, but *a priori*, a new namer. Someone capable of pulling that *something so much more* out of a body – a life – that she'd always considered as *something so much less*.

But, of course, it had led nowhere. It had led from one fictive experience to another. From the *commedia* of one Thursday to the next. Fallows was well aware, now, that only his own fiction could put an end to hers. Bring her flush – in fact – with that mirror. That image in which – indeed – she might finally bathe.

Almost invariably, on the fifteenth of August (on – that is – the day of the Assumption), a violent thunderstorm strikes Provence. It rains – often hails – without relief for six, seven hours consecutively, not only pelting but perforating the vine leaves, and creating a jagged network of ditches where – moments earlier – there'd been only soft ploughings. Most of all, though, the storm marks the end of high summer. Its heavy, lead-white rain draws a curtain, in a sense, across two months of blazing heat, and pulls open another. For just after come the first, alleviating breezes, and – along with them – a washed, revivified light. In only a matter of hours, the realm of the fixed cicada gives way to that – ambient – of the speckled grasshopper.

That year, the fifteenth fell on a Thursday. Well ahead of the time they'd agreed upon, Guy Fallows arrived at an *auberge* that lay at the far end of a long avenue of plane trees. It appeared as if buried in so much dishevelled lilac. In the aftermath of the storm, the air was already cool, and the sky perfectly clear. Off the tall, overhanging trees, rain still dropped, and the drive itself was strewn – virtually carpeted – with so many freshly fallen leaves. The leaves made a slapping sound as they wrapped about the tyres of Guy Fallows's glistening, black Citroën. He parked and entered.

Inside, he was shown to a low bedroom with a dark, beamed ceiling. At right angles to the beams, black rafters ran as if sandwiched between wedges of white plaster. The bed was wide, Fallows noted, and the two armchairs thickly upholstered. He wanted to make himself as familiar as he could with the particularities of that space: that 'setting', as he called it. For within an hour or so, it would become (small as it might appear) the stage upon which their entire relationship would turn. Transform itself, Fallows felt virtually convinced.

'Wait,' she'd say, he knew perfectly well.

'Wait, wait,' she'd beg, over and over, fully aware that her own identity – Frédérique's very existence, as such – was at stake. That Frédérique herself would vanish in the very mirror that Guy Fallows had been quietly preparing, now, month after month.

She arrived late, looking blanched, distraught. As if – Fallows remarked – she'd already anticipated what was about to happen. She turned, hesitated, couldn't decide, for instance, which hanger to hang her coat on, or which of the two armchairs to wrap herself up in. There was never any question, what's more, of the bed. As to what she'd like ordered from the bar, she finally answered, distractedly, 'Whatever. It doesn't really matter. You decide.'

When she'd finally settled, though, in one of those armchairs, Fallows went ahead (as he had how many

124

times previously), and proposed to read from his novel. This time, however, she seemed – surprisingly enough – to acquiesce. If she didn't accept, she didn't refuse, either. Didn't say, 'Wait.' Didn't try to postpone – by every pretext imaginable – what she must have recognized, now, as something utterly unavoidable. It was as if she, too, had come to the same realization that their fictive life, together, was reaching its end. And that *something*, indeed, had to happen. *Something* soon. That the waiting – for better or worse – had ended.

So, as she sipped at a whisky, curled up in her deep armchair, he began reading. They'd ordered a whole bottle of 'Cutty Sark', in fact, so as he read – chapter after chapter – he'd hear her, from time to time, pour herself a fresh drink. Hear the ice-cubes as they clicked dully against the tall glass, then gradually – as the glass went empty – rattle at its very base.

He began at the beginning: read of Marguerite St Chamas's demand, and of Guido's dilemma. How that dilemma was solved – *ipso facto* – by the sheer spectacle of Marguerite St Chamas's rich, unfastened hair. It had filled Guido with 'the demon of irresistibility', and – from that day forth – bound him to her every wish. Her wishes, at first, were entirely proprietorial: that the dovecote be rebuilt. Out of so much rubble, that it rise – once again – into a solid, reconstituted mass. Along with the tower, however, arose a passion. Neither of them would ever know the extent to which the other (in her – his – own, particular way) would languish. Would lust for the next row's completion. The *pigeonnier*, in a sense, was turning into a stone calendar, marking – row after row – so many nights, weeks, months, of rapturous (if disparate) coition.

Came the child. Came the birth of that little girl to whom Guido felt such an immediate attachment. He, who'd nearly been her father, became, now, the perfect substitute. Whenever he could, he'd whisper, sing, hover over the infant like some ungainly bird over its offspring. By now, in fact, he was rebuilding the tower as much for the child as for her mother. As an offering – in a sense – to both, Guy Fallows read.

Then, came the telegram, the four-word telegram. And – just after – came the father himself, Emmanuel St Chamas, hidden those past two years by French missionaries in West Africa. Hidden, that is, from the inevitable reprisal he'd have to face, sooner or later, for his own, odious crime. (At this point in his narrative, Fallows distinctly heard Frédérique pour herself a fresh drink. Heard the slosh of whisky, then the knock of so many ice-cubes against the glass's tall, slippery flanks. In fact, as he went on reading of the father – of the father's utter ignominy – Fallows would hear, increasingly now, the splash of so much freshly poured whisky, followed by the unmistakable clicking of those slow, orbiting cubes. Would hear – at the same time – the crack of matches, and the nearly imperceptible sigh of so much steady exhalation. The room, gradually, began smelling of Stuyvesants.)

As for Fallows himself, he never looked up. He went on reading, turning the tall pages of his manuscript, more and more assured with each page that here, indeed, was a faithful transcript of reality. Here was something, no matter how distasteful, in which Frédérique might at last recognize herself. Yes, here – finally – was his gift. His greatest gift. Of the first, formative years of her life, here – at long last – was the mirror.

Fallows was well into the chapter, now, that touched upon the final stages of the tower's reconstruction. Guido Stampelli, the substitute father, had already become – in the young girl's eyes – the father-elect. The only father, in fact, she'd ever consider as such. She'd grown quickly, and was old enough, now, to wander down into the meadow, and gather flowers. In Guy Fallows's description, in effect, she would have just returned from the meadow – her apron filled with jonquils – when Frédérique, quite unexpectedly, interrupted. Yes, the little girl was about to offer Guido a fat, chaotic bunch of jonquils – her eyes no higher than the knees of the stone-mason's faded blue trousers – when Frédérique, unexpectedly, asked, 'You like her, don't you?'

Fallows looked up from his manuscript. Taken by surprise, he couldn't quite answer.

'Admit it, you do, don't you?' she urged.

'She must have been a lovely little girl,' Fallows replied, as off-handedly as he could.

'Yes, lovely, indeed. Tell me, do you *still* find her lovely?'

Fallows didn't answer.

'You do, don't you? You've always had – how do they call it? – a kind of yearning for Solange – Solange Daubigny – haven't you?'

Fallows looked across at that taut, distraught figure, facing him. She sat, curled up in the armchair, her tanned legs tucked under a long, blue linen skirt. By the very tips of her fingers, she was holding – against her bright, blonde temple – an empty glass.

She returned his gaze, just then, keeping it – as she did – level with his. Hers, though, was far more penetrating. 'Tell me,' she continued, 'tell me exactly what it is about Solange Daubigny that you find so ... appealing, let's say.'

Fallows didn't answer.

'Tell me. Tell me, Guy,' she insisted. 'I need to know.' Her gaze, momentarily, had dropped. It seemed to shuttle, now, between the whisky bottle and the chromium ice-bucket, both of which sat reflected on the lacquer-topped coffee table. Then, fixing herself a fresh drink, she went on as if addressing the tall glass itself and the ice-cubes she sent swirling through it. 'What is it,' she asked, quite quietly, 'that drives someone like yourself – someone essentially honest – to behave in such a deceitful way? Tell me,' she asked, almost confidentially, 'it's something . . . something I need to know.'

Then, that very instant, her gaze rose to meet his. Its clear blue had gone a deep, opaque shade of sapphire. 'Using me as you did, for instance. Using me,' she continued, 'and all the while, desiring *her*. What, what is it exactly? Tell me, Guy. Whatever drove you to such a thing?'

Fallows, sitting there, could hear the room – that very moment – fill with a kind of silence. Hear the silence as if spread to its very corners. It seemed to crackle, he thought, like dry tissue. Or so much static from some distant station.

'All those months,' she went on, still quietly. 'Those Thursdays. All those gorgeous Thursdays when you called me Frédérique, your Frédérique, and took me under. Plundered me, over and over, took me for everything I had, didn't you, when it wasn't me. Wasn't me,' she said, her voice rising now. 'Wasn't me you wanted, at all, was it?'

As her voice rose, Fallows heard the silence grow even louder, beating now – like dry waves – inside his eardrums.

'Was it?' she began to shriek. 'Was it? Wasn't me, at all, was it? *Ce n'était pas du tout moi que tu baisais.* Wasn't me, wasn't me, at all, you were fucking, was it?

'Was it?

'Well, was it?' Her shrieks echoed through that silence far louder than any sound she might have made. Went on echoing, in fact, well after the two of them – quite separately – had left that low bedroom with its beamed

128

ceiling. Had abandoned, altogether, that *auberge* which lay as if buried in so much storm-tossed lilac.

Went on echoing through that silence – far louder than any sound – well after they'd driven off, first one, then the other, in totally distinct – opposing – directions.

14

From that day forth, the tower began to crumble, collapse. The words, the patiently constructed paragraphs that – page after page – Guy Fallows had been assembling like so many limestone blocks, no longer rose, now, towards completion. Had no one – nothing – to rise toward. For whom to gather in a single, turgid vertical of pure offering. No, it had all begun to slip, dissolve. To lose all sense of its own necessity. Even the completed chapters of *The Pigeonnier* had begun falling – for Guy Fallows – into sheer inconsequence. For, along with everything else in his life, Fallows – quite suddenly – had lost heart.

What's more, the tower was not only crumbling, collapsing, but – bit by bit – engendering a kind of anti-tower of its own. A hole of sorts. A deep, embedded depression. What had once risen, had now fallen to a level even lower than that of its own rubble. The tower, in effect, had begun growing, in Guy Fallows's mind, downwards. Forming a kind of replica in negative. He entered its darkness, now, as he'd all too recently thrived in its light. There wasn't any direction left.

He'd failed, he knew. In failing Frédérique (for whom the tower, the whole novel, the very surge of his inspiration had been directed) he'd failed himself. There'd be – he realized

– no stasis now. What hadn't risen would go on falling. With each day, plummet deeper and deeper.

He'd begun drinking again. By drinking heavily, eating little, and no longer writing at all, he had the sensation (yes, with each day, more and more) of being wrapped – embalmed – in his own shadows. The light, the lustre, the mystery in things, all lay – suddenly – as if extinguished. What had once given to everything else its value, its meaning, no longer seemed to exist now. He'd found it, years earlier. Then, in nearly no time, had lost it, lost it like the features on those clay faces, dissolving in the rain. Then, twenty years later, had rediscovered it – stunningly, and for a very last time – in the form of Frédérique. In her, or about her, or at the mere mention of her name, Fallows had felt – sometimes for hours at a time – entirely detached from himself. He'd existed as if within her. He'd not only projected, he'd poured so much of his being into her very person that, occasionally, when she'd glance, he'd swear that he'd see – in the heart of that glance, at its very core, as if irrigating the glance itself, giving it its incommensurable quality – something of himself, glancing back.

That, of course, had ended now. That balance. That infinitely delicate adjustment that sometimes – but so rarely – exists between two beings. That vestige, perhaps, of some divine prerogative (of bodies, so perfectly mingled, so infused, one with the other, that – for hours at a time – they'd be absolved of any personal identity, whatsoever). Yes, that – for Fallows – had ended, now. Since that last Thursday, he'd felt the direction of his own life flow massively – inexorably – backwards. Downwards. Felt the reflux of so many once luminous particles as they darkened, now. Went, like the tower, under. Whatever lay beneath, he knew, had long been expecting him.

He was alone, now, as never before. For the third and what was clearly the last time, Fallows would have to

131

confront, entirely by himself, the possibility of encountering utterly nothing. Of nothingness. Of that dark into which his father had fallen. Of thrashing about in that pit of shadows in which any form of address, response, was categorically excluded. Hadn't Fallows often wondered, in the past, whether love, passion, the fervour of the devout, the self-sacrifices of the ecstatic, hadn't been – at heart – simply the vehicles, the means by which certain, illuminated spirits had sought to attain their own death *outside* themselves? To transcend that very nothingness, and die in the face of image, icon, the breathing figuration of some beloved 'other'?

Leaving, as they did – he added – their towers, in homage? Their restituted dovecotes, as offerings?

If Guy Fallows had gone on to complete his own *pigeonnier* (and, in effect, he left copious notes to exactly that end), he would have described how Guido, over forty years earlier, had completed his. Had come to work, finally, not only full days, but deep into the night as well. How Guido would use the pigeonholes themselves, now, to shelter the lit candles by which he carved, keyed, fitted those large, ungainly blocks into place. Row after row, the interior blossomed, flourished, rose through the ubiquitous pollen of so much unsettled stone dust.

Guido, now, as he worked, had reached such a level of sublimation that he rarely thought, any longer, of Marguerite St Chamas. If he did, though – if that plump, voluptuous figure, occasionally, entered his thoughts – it only fuelled his own efforts, as a stone-mason, even further. His passion had already been as if transformed – transfigured – into its own celebration. (Wasn't it this, Guy Fallows would wonder, so many years later, that gave the tower its appearance of pure weightlessness? That let it float as if free of its mass, informed – as it was – by nothing less buoyant than its own, irrepressible *élan*?)

Remained, now, nothing but the dome itself: but the double, semi-circular vault that – soon enough – would cap the whole, ascendant structure. How Guido had laid into place – with board, rafter and wedge – the intricate hemisphere of his wood coffering. Then, against this, slid his stones into place. Had slid, not laid, for each of them – each *voussoir* – had been carved to joggle with the next: to lock – interlock, like so many vertebrae – into that high, hooded, self-supporting construct that, today, looked less as if it were crafted by a man, than willed – in a single instant – by some demigod.

It was, apparently, on the very last day of the *pigeonnier*'s reconstruction that it happened. Fallows, here and throughout, had drawn his information from living sources, and most especially from those three card players in the café who'd furnished him, from the beginning, with such a first-hand account of Guido's existence. Each had known him personally, and had given Guy a more or less concordant version not only of Guido's life, but of his death, as well. For, on that very last day, setting the very last stone – the keystone – into place, Guido had fallen. He'd been attempting to dress that final block – adjust it in relation to the four, flanking *voussoirs* (the stone itself freshly carved, chiselled in Guido's own, somewhat rudimentary way to form a stout, altogether guileless heart) – when, from his scaffold, he lost footing and fell. Fell – it might be said, quite literally – from his carved heart. Fell and died, instantaneously, upon impact with the stone floor below.

He'd left, however, his keystone locked into place. And his *pigeonnier*, completed.

As for Fallows's, his went on collapsing. Went on hollowing – out of the very ground it had risen from – its

133

proper negative. Its vacuous imprint. It went on doing so as Fallows himself faced the very last days of his own life, and, in them, made what he called his 'provisions'. These, in fact, consisted of a single readjustment to his estate. For Fallows had telephoned his lawyer – an old college friend from America – and asked him to add an amendment, a single amendment to his 'trust instrument', as it was so termed. This, in effect, would stipulate that all principal and interest, effective immediately, be distributed to his son, Andrew.

' "Immediately"?' the lawyer friend fired back over the telephone.

'Immediately,' Fallows answered.

'Do you understand what you're asking for, Guy?'

'Perfectly,' Fallows responded.

'Do you understand what this implies?'

'I wouldn't have asked for it, otherwise,' Fallows told him. 'How long will it take you to get the papers drawn up and sent off? I'll need them,' he added, 'as quickly as possible.'

There was a long pause. Then the lawyer asked in a voice gone gentle, even commiserating, 'There's nothing serious, is there?'

'Nothing at all.'

'I mean, nothing medical,' he went on, almost meekly. 'Doctors, medical reports, you know what I'm saying, Guy.'

'No, nothing at all, I can assure you.'

'Blood tests, too. I mean, all kinds of people are getting it these days. All kinds.'

'If I'd wanted a doctor, I would have gone to one,' Fallows answered, suddenly impatient. 'Now, how long, exactly how long will it take to draft? Draw up?'

Andrew was Guy Fallows's only heir, in any case. But by making him ultimate beneficiary in Guy's own lifetime, Andrew would be saved a considerable amount of punishment in estate taxes. The lawyer promised Guy Fallows that he'd call back that very afternoon, and assured him that he could have an amended trust in Guy's hands within three days.

So, while Fallows waited for the lawyer's call, he went on drinking, staring – as he did – through his open window-doors on to the blue bar of the Luberon, just beyond. Away, he thought. That's it. They'd both be going away. Getting as far – far from here – as anyone possibly could. To realize that vague, that utopian, that all but impossible vision: to travel as far as Patagonia, and settle. To grow 'things', as Andrew had said. 'Grow what?' Guy had asked him. 'Things, things,' his son had replied. 'Something,' he said after a moment's hesitation, 'brimming with all the vitamins on earth.' 'A panacea of sorts,' the father had suggested. 'Yes, just that, exactly: a panacea. We might even call it that, if you wouldn't mind,' the son responded enthusiastically. 'Call it – our hybrid, our yet-to-be-discovered fruit – a "panacea".'

Yes, Fallows kept thinking: away. In the last direction that's left. Getting as far – far from here – as one possibly could. And yes, planting trees once one got there. Going to the earth's very edge, and planting trees.

The boy would need whatever financial support he might get, Fallows realized. And the amendment, he knew, could only help. So he stood there, staring out, watching the late light gather in the deep pleats of the Luberon, and waited for the phone to ring. When it finally did, however, it wasn't the lawyer. Wasn't the lawyer's voice that spoke heatedly through the receiver. No, wasn't that of some distant colleague's that pleaded, 'Couldn't we meet? Even for an hour? It's so important, so essential, Guy. Even for lunch, let's say. For lunch – for instance – tomorrow, oh couldn't we?'

15

Never would Fallows have seen Frédérique so radiant. They'd decided on a small, open-air *bistrot* alongside the river, just where the Sorgue – fresh from its brief, churning fall from the lip of its source – redresses itself. Goes smooth. Chez Philippe, the river looks more like a sheet of glass, slipping – flush – across a slab of malachite. The grain of the malachite, just beneath, seems to knot. To ripple into so many green, guttering eddies.

'I'm sorry,' she said, 'I've behaved unforgivably. I want you to know how deeply sorry I am.' They were seated opposite one another. Below them, in the river, trout, facing upstream, stood stationed like so many dark pennants, their tails fluttering in the current.

Fallows looked across at Frédérique, now, as if he were facing her portrait. Her own, glowing effigy. No, never had he seen her so radiant, so perfectly lovely. Nor – he added – so strangely remote, either. A steady breeze, following the current, had drawn her short hair taut about the sides of her head. It gave to each of her fine-boned features a particularly sleek, swept-back appearance. She looked, altogether, as if she existed, just then, on the surface of some medallion.

'Please,' she said, imploringly. 'Forgive me.'

She took his hand now between both of hers. He felt

immediately, however, from the pressure of those hands –
those fingers – more a message of simple contrition than
that, say, of any manifest affection.

'Of course,' he told her. 'Of course I forgive you.'

She hesitated. 'Are you certain?'

'Of course I'm certain,' he reassured her.

'You're so kind, Guy. So terribly kind.' As she said this,
he felt the pressure of her hands gradually slacken. Felt the
hands themselves – after a moment – work loose. Come
free. They moved about the table, now, arranging a fork
here, a glass there, idling about the rim of a plate, gracious
– Guy Fallows remarked – as young deer at the edge of a
clearing. Then, suddenly decisive, they rose to her temples,
sent their long, slender fingers forking through that bright,
tightly cropped hair. The hair – just then – shivered like
wind-blown wheat.

'Frédérique, *mon exquise*. My beautiful Frédérique.'

'No,' she said, shaking her head ever so slightly. 'No, no
longer.' Her voice had suddenly gone small; her expression,
plaintive.

'No longer?' he asked. His voice, too, was scarcely
audible, now, over the sound of so much running water.

'*Elle est partie, notre Frédérique. Elle est partie bien
loin,*' she said, her words as if slipping with the river,
just below. 'She's left us, our Frédérique. She's gone a
long way away,' she told him. Her hair reflected, that
very instant, not only the heavy, overhanging foliage, but
a sun wobbling – like a bent coin – upon the river's quick,
scarcely rippling surface.

'I wanted Frédérique to last for ever,' he told her.

'Yes, for ever,' she replied, her voice barely audible.
'Frédérique, for ever. Oh yes, so did I, Guy.'

'Where's Frédérique? What's happened, *mon amour*?
Tell me where Frédérique's gone to.'

She pulled out a cigarillo, and lit it with the single

click of a slender gold lighter. Fallows had never seen the gold lighter before. 'That day,' she began, drawing on the cigarillo until the smoke curled – almost sullenly – from her lips, 'that day,' she hesitated, 'when you read . . . read those pages from your *Pigeonnier*, that very afternoon – you must understand – something happened, that's all. Frédérique as if vanished as you read. As if fled.'

'From *what*, though? From *whom*?'

'From you, Guy,' she said quietly. She forced a smile as she said it. 'From that beautiful name you gave her, and then, that day, that very afternoon – with every page you read – refuted, denied. It was like a spell you cast – don't you see? – then shattered.' As she spoke, Fallows watched, with a certain fascination, the smoke of her cigarillo linger about the corners of her mouth; loiter – in so many loose arabesques – at its wet edges.

'Like a mirror, too,' she continued. 'Like some dark mirror in which, each Thursday, she could strip. Could see herself. Yes, at long last, recognize her own, hidden self, oh don't you understand? Shattered, like a mirror,' she said. 'Yes, shattered,' she went on.

Fallows followed the smoke of her cigarillo, now, as it vanished from her lips; got drawn, swept – suddenly – into a gust of wind. 'That's not what I intended,' he told her. 'Not in any way what I meant.'

The woman (whose name, now, was no longer Frédérique) went on as if oblivious. 'Oh, don't think I didn't try, either. Try and stop her. Try and find her, that Thursday night, in whatever way I could. Long after the house was quiet, and everyone asleep, don't think I didn't reach down to touch what a woman touches, and whisper. Whisper "Frédérique", as I worked at this, fondled at that. Kept searching, probing, trying to find just enough sensation to say: "Yes, yes, you're still there, aren't you? Still inside me, aren't you, Frédérique? Still warm, receptive to my every touch." '

At that very instant, she extinguished her half-smoked cigarillo. Tapped it hard into a flat, glass ashtray. As she did, its leaves fell apart. 'No,' she went on without any inflexion, now, whatsoever, 'suddenly, there was no one. She'd left, vanished already, our beautiful Frédérique. Left us, for ever,' she said, staring down at the glass ashtray.

'That's not what I meant,' Fallows repeated. 'Not what I wished. I wanted to *give* you a mirror, not shatter one. I wanted to give you something in which you could see. See to your very depths.'

'No,' she said, flatly. 'You wanted me to return to that farmhouse, that past. Become what I'd once been, that's all. That's all that you wanted,' she muttered, still without the very least inflexion. And, as she did, Fallows felt (more, perhaps, than he ever had before) the full weight of her rejection. How she'd rejected not merely his portrait of her past, but that past itself: that mother who'd scarcely been a mother, and worse – far worse – that father: the unpardonable crime of that unforgivable father.

'And now?' Fallows asked. Dared to ask.

'Now,' she said, as if musing on her own response, 'now, it's simply too early. Too early to say.'

'Too early,' he ventured, 'or too late?'

'A bit, perhaps, of both,' she answered, rather solemnly.

They sat there facing the river, taking occasional forkfuls of that flaking *truite meunière aux amandes* they'd both ordered, but clearly hadn't the appetite, now, to finish. They scarcely touched their *rosé*, that day, either. The sunlight, falling down through the wine glasses, left pale pink ovoids – ellipses – printed across the white tablecloth before them.

'Mirrors,' she murmured, as if to herself alone.

139

'Yes, mirrors,' he responded, and felt – as he did – a sudden, unexpected ripple of pleasure at that tiny accord: that small agreement they'd just had, even if it be only over a single word.

'Maybe it's that, only that. A question of mirrors,' she said, taking a sip, now, of her *rosé*.

'Yes,' Fallows agreed, 'maybe it's only that, indeed.'

'Finding someone in whose eyes one can see – almost read – oneself. A mirror of sorts. Yes, someone in whom – already – I've begun catching glimpses. Not much, but a gesture, here. An intonation – the ring of a certain laughter – there. Yes, already, perhaps. A mirror of sorts.'

Fallows felt her words, her 'someone in whom . . . already . . .' rush through him like the raised tongue of a blowtorch. Felt them sear. They settle nowhere. The 'someone' lapped, now, like fire through his lungs. Then, a moment later, sat as if burning in his innards.

'Yes, already. Finding myself,' the woman explained, 'through another's eyes, feeling myself grow. Grow whole, strong again, don't you see?' she insisted, touching the top of his hand with the palm of hers. 'Oh, don't you, Guy?'

'Of course,' he answered. He could scarcely recognize his own voice, though, as he said it.

'And wouldn't you be the first to rejoice (*réjouir*), seeing me well, once again? "Radiant", as you used to call me, oh, wouldn't you?'

Fallows was staring down at the river, just below, observing how the swollen blue bubbles that the falls had generated drifted, now, with the current downstream. To Fallows, they appeared – that very instant – to be travelling backwards. As if against themselves.

'Yes, of course,' he answered automatically, too stunned to remember exactly what the woman had said. 'Of course,' he murmured, 'of course I would.'

'You'll forgive me, won't you?' she asked.

He nodded, still dazed.

'Both of us, you'll forgive both of us, won't you, Guy?'

Fallows was still staring at the river, at its bubbles. He watched how the bubbles arrived in whole flotillas at a time, bumping slippery – one against the other – before catching, once again, in the swift, green muscles of the current itself. Occasionally, he noticed, one would burst. Would leave, in its place, a white ring, an empty imprint, floating – at the very same, imperturbable speed – downstream.

'Won't you? Won't you, Guy?'

'How can I forgive someone I don't even know?' he asked, sullenly. 'I don't even know him.'

With a voice that could just barely be heard over the rush of the current, the woman uttered, 'What makes you think it's a "him"?'

She pressed her soft palm into his knuckles, now. Pressed it, over and over. 'Won't you? Won't you, Guy?'

Fallows was still staring at the river. He was looking for something within the current to focus upon. To still the rush of his thoughts. He could hear his heart beating, now, a full octave below that of the thudding waterfall, just overhead.

'Whatever,' he finally replied. 'Whatever you wish. Whatever would make you happy.'

'Oh, *that* would,' she said ardently. '*That* would, indeed.'

He looked across at her tanned face – yes, a medallion, an image, a magnificent, blonde effigy of that very woman he'd known and loved. She sat there, just then – Guy Fallows thought – as close as salvation itself. And yet, at the same time – with each passing instant – seemed as if to recede. That very moment, in fact, she'd begun running lipstick over her untouched lips, smearing them together into a perfect imprint, preparing – as she

141

did – to leave. To enter into a world of her own. A world apart.

'Thank you, Guy,' she told him. 'With all my heart, thank you.'

He looked at the fine pencil line of her eyebrows, then at the eyes themselves, the deep scoop of their lashes. He looked at each of these features, now, as if he were in the process of memorizing them.

'You've been so kind. So very, very kind,' she said, leaning over to kiss him – lightly as she could – on each cheek. As she did, Fallows detected, from behind her ears, the scent of some entirely new, somewhat abrasive perfume. No, not a trace of honeysuckle, now, remained.

'Be well,' he whispered.

'Be well, yourself,' she replied, and – in a rustle of linen – was gone.

Alone, now, in the virtually deserted restaurant by the river, the tables cleared and the wind tugging at the corners of the tablecloths, Guy Fallows realized that for over an hour, now, he'd forgotten his own fate. Forgotten that he wouldn't go on sitting there, for ever, watching the river. That the woman he'd once called Frédérique, whose blonde hair had gone green in the reflection of so many sun-dappled chestnut leaves, would no longer sit opposite him, now. No longer press her soft palm into the ridge of his knuckles.

That the one thing – as he'd put it – that gave meaning to everything else, no longer existed.

16

That Saturday, along with so much else, Guy Fallows burnt the unfinished manuscript of *The Pigeonnier*. He'd no longer need the fat sheath of its already completed chapters, not to mention all those copious notes: those *carnets* charged with so much carefully prepared material. In less than a minute, months of work (not to mention a lifetime of craftsmanship) went up through the narrow flue of his fireplace. With scarcely a hiss from the flames themselves, it all vanished.

Fallows, now, had more or less 'put his house in order', as he might have phrased it. He'd returned his amended trust, duly signed and notarized, to his lawyer in America, and written his son a long, explanatory letter. The letter, touching, first, on so many material considerations, went on to wish the boy well in his venture: in *all* his ventures. 'Go,' the father wrote, 'and may every good fortune go with you.' Then, in conclusion, he asked for the son's understanding. Asked – in a language of scarcely checked desperation – for the son's forgiveness.

That afternoon – Fallows's very last – he went about paying bills, burning letters, leaving as little trace of himself as possible. He drank, of course, as he had every afternoon of his life. Drank that dark, hosepipe wine, that *gros rouge* on which he'd virtually nurtured himself over the past twenty years. From time to time, he tried to eat, as well. But he couldn't retain the least thing. For the last five or six days, he'd vomited nearly every solid he'd taken. It's not the food, though, he realized. It's me, myself, I can't any longer hold. No, no longer.

Towards the latter part of that last afternoon, however, towards the hour, that is, the Luberon begins to pleat – its ravines, once again, go violet – Fallows felt a sudden doubt, an acute hesitation. It was something he hadn't at all expected. He'd been, just then, on the point of burning his old address book, chucking it – along with everything else – into the fire, when, instead, he opened it up. Began leafing through it. He'd heard of this happening. Heard that the despondent often turn – at the critical moment – backwards. Start calling this person, then that. Hoping, as they do, for some form of response. Some glint, perhaps off any of those long-lost mirrors. Yes, those long since departed lovers. Their dissolved echoes. Someone who might – at the very last moment – cry 'no' to that which the despondent had already affixed his 'yes'. Cry 'don't', at the very edge of the irreparable.

It was late summer, however, and no one Fallows tried calling, that afternoon, could be reached. H., living with her three children on the upper East Side, was spending the weekend at her house in Southampton. The number, there, was unlisted. It couldn't be given. S., for her part, was taking a cruise down the Danube, that week, and had left – on her answering machine – a tender message for someone called Barry. S., Fallows knew, would have flown to his rescue. Would have dropped everything, on an instant's notice, and – yes – flown. But she wasn't available.

If, at last, he called *her*, it wasn't, first, without considerable hesitation. For they hadn't had any contact, now, for over twelve years. And even then, even that was only a scribble, dashed off hastily on the back of an announcement to an exhibition she was having in some small gallery in Kajaani, Finland. As to the scribble, it was perfectly illegible. He'd kept it, nonetheless, and, along with it, the name and telephone number of the gallery itself. It was there – that number – that Guy Fallows found himself dialling, that afternoon. He hadn't any other. He'd heard that she'd spent the better part of her time moving from one sanatorium to another. From one disintoxication centre to the next. So Fallows himself was prepared for the worst. When, however, he was told by a cheerful male voice with a high, sing-song accent, that she'd died, six, seven years earlier – 'of cirrhosis of the liver, I believe, if I'm not mistaken' – Fallows could only feel himself slip even deeper. Feel the shadows as if gather, in a single instant, that much more.

Could the gallery be of any assistance, the voice went on. Was there any particular sculpture, for example, that he'd like to see? They'd be more than pleased to send photographs, for instance, along with a price list, if he so wished.

Remained, now, one last number. Guy Fallows looked at his watch. At that hour, Maurice Daubigny would – almost certainly – be somewhere in those woods of his. For tomorrow, at dawn, the hunt officially opened. Yes, he'd be searching out, already – Fallows reckoned – those *passages*, those runs that the hustling boar had taken in the past few weeks. Their tracks would still be fresh in the late summer dust, and their scent, keen in the twinging nostrils of Daubigny's hypertonic bassets and porcelains and *bleu de Gascogne*.

Fallows went ahead and dialled. He had to hold the receiver, however, quite some time before someone answered. It was a young woman – the voice of a young woman – who finally did. *'Oui,'* she responded, *'j'écoute.'*

145

'*Est-ce que je peux parler avec Madame Daubigny, s'il vous plaît?*'

'*Un instant,*' she replied, somewhat dryly.

Fallows heard the young woman (whose palm was quite evidently cupped over the mouthpiece) call out for someone called Paule.

'*Paule, c'est pour toi, chérie,*' she said. 'It's for you, Paule, darling.' Then, in a muffled whisper, 'It's a man.'

An instant later, he heard footsteps (the neat clicking of high heels over waxed floor-tiles), then whispers, then the voice of the one whom he – himself – had always called Frédérique.

'Forgive me for calling,' he said. 'It's me. It's Guy. I must see you in private, even for only a moment.'

'I'm sorry,' she answered, obviously embarrassed by the presence of the third, 'but I can't. I simply can't, right now.'

'It's not what you think,' he continued. 'Please, anywhere you say, it's essential.'

'But we've said everything, Guy. Discussed everything that needed to be discussed. No, no, I simply can't.'

'You don't understand.'

'Oh, but I do,' she said.

'Only for a moment,' he pleaded. 'By the cypress hedge, for instance. We needn't talk, I promise you. Needn't say anything, if you prefer.'

'No,' she whispered, almost breathlessly. 'Don't, don't insist, please.'

'Just long enough to *see* you, that's all I'm asking. For only an instant, this afternoon. To *see* you, that's all. I assure you, that's all that I'm asking.'

'Write,' she whispered. She must have been holding her hand against the mouthpiece, now, as she spoke. 'Why don't you write to me?' she asked, still in a whisper. 'You always can, you know. You can always send me a letter here – to the house – if you wish. You know that, Guy, don't you?'

He didn't answer.

'Don't you?' she repeated. Repeated into a silence that, yes, had grown – once again – louder than any sound. Had grown, for Guy Fallows, absolute. For now, he hadn't any more numbers to dial.

17

That night – his very last – he tried to find her. Some time after midnight, he rolled over on to that bright, glowing shaft – that blondness of his own making – and pressed himself hard against it. Shoved himself, over and over, against so much chimera. He'd entered the hollow, now, of his own heart. The draught of his own shadows. Had he found her, of course, he might – in the same moment – have found himself. But no, there was no one, now. Hard as he pressed, he found nothing. Over and over, nothing but the drained mirror of what had once – for a single, last, beautiful summer – been but a final glimpse of himself.

For locked inside the wet parts of that living reflection, he'd been able – at long last – to reclaim something he'd lost. After so many years, been able to recognize, against those contours, his own.

That night, he went on grappling. Ran his knee – just then – against no one's side. Against no one's damp, lacquered flanks. Pinned, under his own shoulders – now – nothing if not the ripple of so much stale linen. But the formless bulk of his own, exhausted pillows. And, as he did, his mouth would open and close, open and close. Muttering – all the while – perfectly nothing.

*

In another age – under another sign – it might have been said that Guy Fallows was wrestling for his own name. Was tangling – say – with some angel. Struggling for that word which would have vouched for his own. The angel – however – had long since vanished. And with it, that word, that sound, that reflection which once gave – to all others – its sustenance.

Guido, of course, might have been that word.

Guido, whom Guy kept calling. Kept calling in his sleep, as later, much later that night, he dreamt of pigeons. As, towards dawn, he saw the pigeons settle, flutter down on to the cornice and stone mouldings of that *pigeonnier* that Guido Stampelli had built for Marguerite St Chamas, over forty years earlier. Heard, in the same moment, the dull thunder of so much wingbeat. So much white, ruffling plumage. Yes, as they settled, over and under and against one another, forming – as they did – a single, luminous fabric. A throbbing weave of uninterrupted whiteness.

'Guido,' he'd called out.

'Guido,' he'd uttered, as if testing the sound of those two, sharp syllables against that of the muffled air, all about him. Yes, testing. Trying them, as one might try a particular key in a totally strange keyhole. Try, though, as hard as he might – teasing the bit of those two syllables against so much irresponsive metal – the key wouldn't work. The door – whatever the door might be – wouldn't open. The room, the garden, the fountain – whatever it was that lay on the opposite side – would, for Guy Fallows, remain, now, forever inaccessible.

'Guido, Guido,' he went on crying, nonetheless. Hollering into the very heart of his white dream. Of all words, it would – indeed – be his very last.

The rest, he knew – once he'd awakened – would be relatively simple. Would be a matter of eliminating every other consideration from his mind but that. But the act, itself. Would be a matter of entering – expeditiously as possible – that rite, that ritual, as he might have called it. What, in a single lifetime, could be enacted but once.

The wind, he felt, would be in his favour. He'd heard it, even in his dreams, growing – as mistrals will – out of some dark, invisible socket, well before dawn. Now, as he dressed (fastening his shirt buttons, he realized, for the very last time), he listened to the branches of an oak, just overhead. In the wind, the oak was scrubbing against the roof-tiles, sending an acorn, occasionally, scuttling down the dry gutters. The stars, he knew, would be enormous, now. Even a full hour before dawn, they'd be wobbling – brilliant – in their stations. Would go on burning, too, until the sky – in so many steady, chromatic gradations – had thoroughly blanched.

He wouldn't shave, he'd decided. He wouldn't give off any odour that the dogs – by mischance – might detect as human. They'd already be waiting, too, he realized. Be shivering in place, not from the cold (it was scarcely cool at that hour), but from an excitement – an excitement compounded by ten months of unchecked anticipation – over the opening of the hunt. For, within an hour, it would commence. And the dogs, Guy Fallows feared, being highly strung and especially sensitive that day, could – potentially – give away that particular rite. Yes, that ritual of his, as he might have called it.

No, he wouldn't shave, he'd decided. Wouldn't have to face, furthermore, that stranger's face: that querulous gaze that met his, each time he'd looked into a mirror. That constant inquisition. No, now he was no one. Was free, at last, to become nothing. What's more, he'd be wearing his oldest clothes, still redolent of mushrooms and juniper, of the sharp, acidic needles of the shaggy aleppo. He'd be smelling as much like *they* did, he'd decided, as he possibly could. Because soon, he'd be taking the very paths, the very passages that *they'd take*, and which hunters such as Maurice Daubigny had staked out, days earlier. On either side, already, those hunters would have established their posts, stationing the various members of their party (each with their own, innumerable dogs) at one clearing after another. So that now, already, anything bounding up along those paths (the paths no wider than the rushing flanks themselves, oily as axle grease and brown as calamander wood) would not only not escape detection, but would receive an immediate – and mortal – concentration of fire. For, at regular intervals, the hunters would have already trained their breech-loaded, double-barrelled rifles on so much wind-shuffled foliage, waiting – at each instant – for that sudden eruption. For the pig itself – cunning as a fox and silent as its own shadow – to emerge. Emerge, and, in the very same instant – caught in so much cross-hair – turn against the fire that, no longer locked in the barrel of a shotgun, was wedged, now, somewhere behind its forehead. To turn and fall, now, in a bristling mass, as far as thirty metres from the very point at which – an instant earlier – it had, in fact, been felled.

The wind, indeed, would be in Guy Fallows's favour. It would cover the sound of his own footsteps as he came down the narrow path between two overhanging vineyards (trellised to the same height as himself) and headed towards the dark woods, just before him. The wind, in fact, had already set up such a confusion of leaves and branches in the undergrowth that it would have been virtually impossible, at that hour, to differentiate – even from a short distance – a rapidly moving human being from any other, full-size mammal. The wind, in so much boxwood and dark, glistening ilex, created – altogether – a near-perfect camouflage.

Fallows would still, perhaps, be murmuring 'Guido' as

he approached those woods. As, just ahead, he'd hear –
even through the roar of the wind – dogs barking and
the beaters calling out. He might, on the other hand,
have already abandoned that last word altogether. That
final mutter. Might have let it go like some spent token.
Some dissolved, forgotten wafer. Might have prepared himself to enter the woods – that very instant – wordlessly.

Dawn, just then, would be breaking, and the very last
stars quivering, as if against their own extinction. Ahead,
he knew, would be the hunters. They'd be lying in wait with
their double-barrelled Brownings and Winchesters, and –
for the wealthier – those astonishingly light, hand-carved,
fancifully scrolled Chapius's, trained – safeties released –
upon the path, the spoor before them. They'd be firing now
on any even slightly suspect movement, releasing – as they
did – those double, number nine cartridges, charged with
pellets big – say – as chickpeas or periwinkles.

No, as he prepared to enter the woods, Guy Fallows
wouldn't be whistling. Wouldn't be murmuring. All that
mattered, he realized, was not to be mistaken, now, for
what he actually was. Bunching his shoulders together,
he'd crouch, now, and plunge – fast as he could – into
the undergrowth ahead.

A NOTE ON THE AUTHOR

Author of a novel, *Venus Blue*, and many volumes
of poetry, Gustaf Sobin has spent thirty years living
in France.